The
Two Princesses
of Bamarre

Also by
GAIL CARSON LEVINE

Ella Enchanted

Dave at Night

The Wish

THE PRINCESS TALES
The Princess Test
The Fairy's Mistake
Princess Sonora and the Long Sleep
Cinderellis and the Glass Hill
For Biddle's Sake
The Fairy's Return

The Two Princesses of Bamarre

GAIL CARSON LEVINE

AN IMPRINT OF HARPERCOLLINSPUBLISHERS

Eos is an imprint of HarperCollins Publishers.

The Two Princesses of Bamarre
Copyright © 2001 by Gail Carson Levine
Library of Congress Cataloging-in-Publication Data
Levine, Gail Carson.
  The two princesses of Bamarre / by Gail Carson Levine.
    p.   cm.
  Summary: With her adventurous sister, Meryl, suffering
from the Gray Death, meek and timid Princess Addie sets out
to find a cure.
  ISBN 0-06-029315-2 — ISBN 0-06-029316-0 (lib. bdg.)
  ISBN 0-06-440966-X (pbk.) — ISBN 0-06-057580-8 (pbk.)
  [1. Princesses—Fiction.   2. Wizards—Fiction.   3. Magic—
Fiction.   4. Sisters—Fiction.   5. Self-confidence—Fiction.]
I. Title.
PZ7.L578345 Tw 2001   00-047953
[Fic]—dc21   CIP
                                                    AC

❖

First Eos edition, 2004
Visit us on the World Wide Web!
www.harpereos.com

To Joan Abelove,
my pal on this fine wild ride
—a million thanks
—G.C.L.

The Two Princesses of Bamarre

Chapter One

Out of a land laid waste
To a land untamed,
Monster ridden,
The lad Drualt led
A ruined, ragtag band.
In his arms, tenderly,
He carried Bruce,
The child king,
First ruler of Bamarre.

So begins *Drualt*, the epic poem of Bamarre's greatest hero, our kingdom's ideal. Drualt fought Bamarre's monsters—the ogres, gryphons, specters, and dragons that still plague us—and he helped his sovereign found our kingdom.

Today Bamarre needed a hero more than ever. The monsters were slaughtering hundreds of Bamarrians every year, and the Gray Death carried away even more.

I was no hero. The dearest wishes of my heart were for safety and tranquility. The world was a perilous place, wrong for the likes of me.

Once, when I was four years old and playing in the castle courtyard, a shadow passed over me. I shrieked, certain it was a gryphon or a dragon. My sister, Meryl, ran to me and held me, her arms barely long enough to go around me.

"It's gone, Addie," she whispered. "It's far away by now." And then she crooned a stanza from *Drualt*.

> *"Step follows step.*
> *Hope follows courage.*
> *Set your face toward danger.*
> *Set your heart on victory."*

I quieted, soothed by Meryl's voice and her warm breath on my ear.

Meryl was my protector, as necessary to me as air and food. Our mother, Queen Daria, had succumbed to the Gray Death when I was two and Meryl was three. Father rarely visited the nursery. Bella, our governess, loved us in her way, but her way was to moralize and to scold.

Meryl understood me, although we were as different as could be. She was fair, and I was dark complexioned. She was small and compact, a concentration of focused energy. I was always tall for my age, and loose-limbed, and my energy was nervous and fluttery. Meryl was brave, and I was afraid of almost everything—from monsters to strangers to spiders.

As a child Meryl loved to act out scenes from *Drualt* or scenes from a made-up drama in which she saved the kingdom. Our games would begin on the miniature carriage that was our nursery's best feature. I'd sit inside, and Meryl would climb up to the driver's seat. We'd travel to the Eskern Mountains, where ogres and gryphons dwelled, or to the elf queen's castle on the shores of the Haun Ocean, or to the western desert, where the dragons had their lairs, or to Mulee Forest, where specters abounded.

She would rescue me from a flaming dragon or a hungry ogre. When I was supposed to, I would shriek in terror that was half real; but when I could, I'd stay still and watch Meryl perform—that was what I loved.

Her favorite game was the Gray Death adventure. Oddly enough this one didn't frighten me. The Gray Death wasn't a monster or a spider I could see and shiver over. It was invisible. If I caught it, it would be somewhere within me, and while the outside world was full of danger, I knew my interior. I was certain I could oust an intruder there.

In the game I always portrayed the Gray

Death's victim. For the first stage of the disease, the weakness, I'd begin to walk toward the worn nursery couch, growing weaker as I went. After a few steps I'd fall to my knees and begin to crawl. I'd drag myself to the couch but lack the strength to climb up onto it.

I'd fall asleep there on the floor. A moment or two later I'd wake up and rise, consumed by fever. I'd rush to the fireplace and rub ashes into my cheeks, because the faces of the afflicted always turned gray near the end. I'd pretend to shiver, and I'd try to make my teeth chatter.

Meanwhile, Meryl would be busy battling monsters, consulting with sorcerers, climbing mountains, sailing stormy seas. While I shivered, I'd keep one eye on her, because I couldn't start to die until she was ready to rescue me. When she triumphed and found the cure, I'd slump to the floor.

She'd rush to me, cradling the cure in both hands. Sometimes it was an elixir in a golden chalice. Sometimes it was the feather of a gryphon or the tooth of a dragon or even a plain black stone. Kneeling at my side, she'd whisper, "I have found it, maiden. You shall live." She'd cure me, and I'd jump up. Then we'd frolic about the nursery, skipping around the carriage, banging on the suit of armor, clasping hands and dancing around the small spinning wheel.

We knew that a cure would be found one day. A specter had prophesied it, and the prophecies of specters always came true. The cure would be found *when cowards found courage and rain fell over all Bamarre*. That was all we knew. No one knew when the cure would be found, by whom, or what form it would take.

Once, at the end of our game, I asked Meryl if she really planned to quest for the cure. I was nine at the time, and Meryl was ten.

"I'll leave as soon as I'm strong enough to ride a charger."

She'd never come back! A monster would kill her.

She took a heroic stance, legs apart, brandishing an imaginary sword. "I'll find the cure, and knights will flock to me. We'll destroy the monsters and save Bamarre. Then I'll return home."

She wouldn't. She'd be dead. But I knew better than to say so. Instead I asked, "What will I do while you're away?"

She lowered her pretend sword and smiled. "Why, you'll be the wife of a handsome prince and mother of a little princess who is learning to embroider as beautifully as you do."

I didn't smile back. "What if the prince hasn't come yet, or he didn't like me and left?"

"Then you'll come with me."

"No, I won't. I'd be too afraid. You know I would."

She sighed, exasperated. "Oh, Addie! Suppose I say that I won't go anywhere until you are wed and happy. Does that suit you?"

"Promise?"

She dropped to one knee. "I swear that I shall remain at Bamarre castle until the princess Adelina is wed to her true love. May my sword turn against me if I break this pledge."

"Thank you." I collapsed on the nursery floor, feeling vast relief. Marriage was years and years away.

She threw herself down next to me. We lay quietly for a moment, looking up at the wooden ceiling.

"If I ever really caught the Gray Death," I said, "even if you hadn't found the cure yet, I wouldn't die."

Meryl rolled over. "Why not?"

"Because I wouldn't give in to it. When the disease made me feel tired, I wouldn't act tired. When it made me want to sleep, I'd stay awake. If the fever still came, I'd run up and down to keep myself warm. By refusing to do the Gray Death's bidding, I'd chase the illness away."

Meryl leaped up. "I'd do something hard—climb a mountain, catch an ogre."

I rose and sat on our couch. "I don't know why they die."

She sat too. "I don't know why anybody dies, except when they're burned to a crisp by a dragon or skewered by a valiant knight." She thought for a moment and then shrugged. "I *will* find the cure, you know."

I nodded. "But if I become ill before then, I won't fall prey to death."

Chapter Two

When I was twelve, my chambermaid, Trina, contracted the Gray Death. It was the first time I saw the disease at close quarters. A few people in the castle died of it every year, but I'd never known any of them well.

Before she took sick, Trina used to snap the bedclothes off my bed in the morning and shake them sharply. She was a grumpy angular woman, and all her gestures were sharp.

Then one morning there was no snap in her. She took away my bedclothes, moving as if she were swimming through syrup.

Later that day our governess, Bella, who heard all the castle gossip, told Meryl and me that the elf nurses were tending Trina. An elf had seen her in a corridor and had noticed her loose stride. Only her stride, and the elf knew.

Trina had been my chambermaid since I was three. Mornings wouldn't be the same without her grumpiness. I loved her, as I loved all the routines and fixtures of my life.

Since I believed I knew how to defeat the

Gray Death, I wanted to save her. When our lessons with Bella were over, I begged Meryl to come with me to Trina's bedchamber in the west wing. Meryl would be more persuasive than I, and Trina would listen to her.

"I was going to practice my swordplay," Meryl said, frowning. "You can convince her as well as I can."

I shook my head. "She won't do—"

"Better, even. After all, she knows you best." But in the end she agreed to come for a little while.

Milton, an elf nurse, sat next to Trina's bed, knitting. When we came in, he slid off his chair and bowed and smiled at us. Then he sat down again, standing on tiptoe to place himself in the seat. He was the elf we knew best. He had nursed us through colds and sore throats for as long as I could remember.

Meryl strode across the room. "Greetings, Trina!" She took the chair next to the fireplace.

I remained in the doorway for a moment. Someone had put flowers on the mantelpiece— anemones, thought to bring peace to the dying.

It was odd to see Trina clad in a nightdress. She got out of bed to curtsy and didn't seem much weakened yet. Some people weakened quickly, while others remained relatively strong for months. I hoped for Trina to have months to fight the disease.

The second stage, the slumber, always lasted nine days, and the fever always lasted three days and ended in death. If Trina was to have time, it would be in this first stage, the weakness.

Trina climbed back into bed. I started toward the window seat, then froze. A spider was crawling up one of the legs of Trina's bed.

Meryl said, "Addie tells me—"

"Meryl!" My voice was a squeak. I pointed. My heart was pounding. It was a hairy one, the kind I feared most. I wanted to bolt, but I was afraid it would come after me.

Trina raised herself on one elbow. "What's amiss?"

"I see it, Addie." Meryl hurried to the bed and brushed the spider onto her left hand. With her right she cranked open the casement window. I couldn't see, but I knew she was placing the spider on the castle wall. "There." She closed the window.

"What was that?" Trina asked suspiciously.

"Addie tells me you're not feeling well," Meryl said, not answering.

Trina looked straight at me. "It was a spider, wasn't it, Princess Adelina? Begging your pardon, but everyone knows you fear them."

My face heated up as I crossed the room and sat in the window seat. The whole castle probably thought me a worse coward than Father. I glanced over at Milton, but he was knitting placidly and didn't look up.

"No spider," Meryl said. "It's just a game Princess Addie and I play sometimes."

Trina let her head fall back on the pillow. "It was a spider."

"What is your illness, Trina?" Meryl asked. "Has Milton mentioned its name?"

That was clever. I would never have gotten to the subject so quickly, and it was tactful of her to ask Trina rather than Milton.

"He says I have the Gray Death, Your Highness, but he's wrong. I would feel worse if I had it, wouldn't I?"

"I suppose. Then you don't need to know what Princess Addie and I came here to tell you."

"Tell me what?" Trina said. "Begging your pardon."

"That Princess Addie knows how to defeat the Gray Death."

"I told you, I don't have the Gray Death. I'll be better tomorrow."

"You can be better today using Princess Addie's plan."

Trina turned her face to the wall. "I don't have the Gray Death."

Meryl's expression was the same as when her stallion, Bane, turned balky. With Bane she'd apply her spurs and a flick of the whip. With Trina she said, "I command you to listen to Princess Addie's plan."

Trina didn't refuse. She only moved her head to another spot on her pillow and said, "This pillow is too hard. I should have a better one since I'm sick."

Milton stood. "I'll find a better one for you."

Meryl jumped up. "I'm leaving too. I hope you are better soon, Trina."

"I'll stay awhile." I was disappointed in Meryl. But Trina hadn't been her chambermaid, and it wasn't up to Meryl to save her.

After they left, I moved to Milton's chair and pulled it close to the bed. I cast about for the right words.

"Don't expect me to entertain you, Your Highness."

"No," I said, surprised. "I don't expect that." I had an idea. "I dreamed about my mother last night."

"The old queen," Trina said, still facing away and not sounding at all interested.

"That's right." I leaned forward. "Do you know what she told me?"

No answer.

"She said she misses being alive."

"Being queen. That's what she misses, Your Highness. Begging your pardon."

"And do you know what else she said?"

No answer.

"She said that she could have cured herself if she'd struggled. She said, 'Addie, the Gray Death was there, in my chest. If I'd sought it, I would have found it.'"

Trina rolled over and looked at me.

Encouraged, I went on. "She said, 'I could have cast it out.'"

Trina wet her lips to speak.

I waited.

"You're a pretty one," she said. "I always thought so. High smooth brow, fine eyes. Narrow boned. Pretty."

"Thank you." Hadn't she heard anything I'd said?

"You should wear brighter colors, begging your pardon."

I nodded. I loved strong hues in my embroidery and on other people, but not on me.

I returned to saving Trina. "Mother wished

13

she had gone on ruling despite the disease. Perhaps I had that dream so I could tell you to do what Queen Daria said."

Trina's lips twitched. "To go on ruling?"

For a startled moment I wondered if the Gray Death gave people a sense of humor. I smiled. "No, you should do what you always do. Don't let the disease stop you."

"You want to keep your chambermaid, Princess Adelina. Begging your pardon."

I wanted her to live! And I wanted to prove that the Gray Death could be vanquished. "No, I want to help you get well."

Milton entered, carrying two pillows. Someone followed him in—Rhys, our new apprentice sorcerer.

I jumped up. My chair shot out behind me and fell over. In confusion I bent to right it, but Rhys was already there. He picked up the chair and swept me the deepest bow with the most flourishes I'd ever seen.

I curtsied, feeling awkward. He'd come only a week ago. I'd seen him in the banquet hall, but Father hadn't yet thought to introduce him to Meryl and me.

Milton placed the new pillows under Trina's head.

The sorcerer said, "Mistress Trina, I am very sorry that you're feeling ill. Please let me know if there's anything I can do to make you more comfortable."

"I don't want any magic potions, begging your pardon, sir."

Rhys bowed again. "No magic potions. I promise." He smiled.

I felt a jot more at ease. His smile was kind.

He was tall, as sorcerers are. His face was almost flat, with wide cheeks and high cheekbones. His eyes were compelling—large and blue, and ringed by the thick white lashes all sorcerers have. His attire was gay—a brocade doublet and purple satin breeches. Father's last apprentice sorcerer had worn only dark tones. I'd thought drab attire as much a rule with sorcerers as it was with me.

"These pillows are hard too."

Rhys said, "Perhaps I can improve on them." He turned to Milton. "May I try?"

"Go ahead."

Trina sat up straight again, looking alarmed. "I don't want a magic pillow that will explode or fly me away in the middle of the night."

The sorcerer's eyes widened. "I would never

15

give anyone such a pillow." He opened a pouch at his waist, took out a golden baton, and pointed it at the sky.

The afternoon was cloudy. A wisp of white shredded off a cloud and sailed down to the castle, toward us. Rhys opened the window and swept the wisp in with a grand gesture.

A cloud was in the room with us!

Trina put both hands over her face. "Don't let it hurt me!"

Using his baton, Rhys gathered the cloud and shaped it into a pillow.

I began to smile. Trina peeked between her fingers. Milton stood up to see better.

"Sleep is always sweet when your pillow is a cloud." Rhys stepped to her bedside. "Lean forward."

"You're sure it's safe?"

"Perfectly safe."

She did as she was directed, and Rhys placed the cloud pillow behind her. I could see that his touch was gentle.

"There," he said. "Now lean back."

"I'll go right through it!" She lowered her back gingerly while scowling at Rhys. The scowl vanished. "It *is* a trifle better."

"Why, look at that!" Milton said.

I laughed, and spoke before I could think. "The pillow won't rain, will it?"

Rhys laughed too, harder than I had. "Rain! I never thought of that. Pillow rain." He shook his head, still chuckling. "It won't rain, and Trina's dreams will be lovely."

She sighed deeply and closed her eyes. "I think I'll take a nap now."

I didn't want her to nap. I wanted her to listen to me. I appealed to Milton. "Trina should struggle against the Gray Death, shouldn't she?"

"It can't hurt her to try, but she should sleep now. She won't get much rest tomorrow."

I must have looked puzzled, because he added, "One of your father's carriages will take her home to her family tomorrow." He tucked the blanket in around her. "Trina, you'll think over Her Highness's suggestions in the carriage, won't you?"

She nodded with her eyes still closed. I supposed that was something. But I wished I could slip into her cloud-sweetened dreams and persuade her there.

Chapter Three

Rhys walked down the corridor with me. "Your Highness, I see your beautiful embroidery everywhere I look in the castle. I'm so happy to meet the artist."

"Thank you," I murmured. "They're not very good."

"But they're *very* good."

I felt myself blush. I didn't say anything, and we were silent for a few moments.

Then he said, "Making cloud pillows is one of the first lessons a sorcerer learns."

I wondered what the others were, but I was too shy to ask. He was a beginner, as all our sorcerers were. They could fly, of course. All sorcerers could. Their training included five years in the service of a king, for whom they performed minor magic, did simple tricks with the weather, and kept the castle free of rats.

If he could keep rats away . . .

"I'm sorry about your chambermaid." Rhys sighed, an elaborate exhale. "I suppose it's silly to feel sad over someone I hardly know, but you see, sorcerers don't get sick. We're never ill, so illness seems tragic to me." He waited for me to say something.

"Er . . . that's interesting."

We reached the winding stone stairs that descended to the lower floors of the castle. The stairs were too narrow for us to go down side by side, so Rhys chivalrously went first. He looked over his shoulder to continue the conversation. "It *is* interesting. It's interesting how different we are from other creatures—how different we are from humans, and how different humans are from elves and elves are from dwarfs and dwarfs from sorcerers. It's fascinating." He smiled, then frowned. "Are you afraid of becoming a victim of the Gray Death?"

I shook my head.

"You're brave, Princess Addie."

No one had ever called me brave before. It made me feel strange, as if I were impersonating someone, as if Rhys had mixed me up with Meryl.

"Do you think . . . " I hesitated, then said in a rush, "Could you rid the castle of spiders?" He wouldn't think me brave now.

He stopped, and I almost crashed into him. "I think I can." He paused, then nodded vigorously. "Certainly I can." He turned all the way around. "I'll do it tonight. Ugly little beasts, aren't they?"

He didn't like them either!

He started down the stairs again. I smiled at his back. "Thank you."

He stopped and turned again. "You're welcome." He bowed, managing to be dramatic, even in the cramped stairwell.

I had to curtsy too, and then we set off again.

After a few steps he said over his shoulder, "In sorcerers' years I'm a bit older than you are, but not a great deal older. I'm seventy-eight. If I were human, I'd be just about seventeen."

Seventeen at seventy-eight! How long did they live?

"I envy human children. You learn everything you need to know so quickly. We can speak and even fly when we're born, but beyond that we learn almost too slowly to bear."

We reached the bottom of the stairs.

He bowed yet again. "I must leave you now. I look forward to speaking with you again."

He did? So did I!

Back in the nursery Bella was alone, crocheting. I picked up my embroidery, but I was too distracted to work on it. My thoughts kept revolving from Trina to Rhys to no more spiders and back to Trina again.

In half an hour Meryl came in from her swordplay and stood at my shoulder, looking down at my work. She laughed. "I like that! What made you think of it?"

Usually I embroidered scenes from *Drualt*, but this embroidery showed a close view of one of the dozens of gargoyles that adorned Bamarre castle. The rest of the castle was visible in the background—the coral-colored stone walls, the blue tower roofs, the slitted upper windows, and the vaulting arches between tower and buttress.

The gargoyle in the foreground was a gryphon's head, with fierce bulging eyes and a bone in its cruel beak. Next to it a real gryphon hovered in the air, its beak hanging open in astonishment. The real monster appeared much less dangerous than its twin in stone.

"I don't know why I thought of it," I said. But I did know. I had invented the scene to comfort myself, to tame one monster at least.

I changed the subject. "Has anyone ever caught the Gray Death and lived?"

Bella answered, "Your father hears about

cures now and then, but it always turns out that the person didn't have the Gray Death in the first place."

"Do you think the fairies could cure Trina?" I said.

"I have no idea."

"Bella!" Meryl said. "Certainly the fairies can cure the Gray Death. They can do anything." She picked up her thick book about battles with monsters and sat in our gilded throne chair.

Fairies hadn't been seen by humans for hundreds of years. They were believed to have retreated to their home atop the invisible Mount Ziriat. They still visited the elves and sorcerers and dwarfs occasionally, but never humans.

They were sorely missed. We used to have fairy godfathers and godmothers. Fairies had known our best selves better than anyone else, and they'd encouraged us and given us a boost when we were in trouble. There were fairies in *Drualt*, and the hero himself was believed to have visited them on Mount Ziriat. But that might have been fable. We had no certainty about any of Drualt's life—or even whether he'd lived or not. He might have been merely the invention of a long-ago anonymous bard.

Meryl said, "Someday I'll find the fairies and persuade them to come back to us. If I haven't found the cure by then, I'll get it from them." She turned a page in her book. "Addie . . . do you want me to search for them now so they can save Trina?"

My heart skipped a beat. No! No, I didn't want her to search. I didn't want her to go anywhere.

Bella exploded. "Search for fairies! You're a princess. Not a knight, not a soldier, a princess!"

"Do you want me to, Addie?"

"No," I said quickly. "I think Trina will rescue herself. She promised to consider my method." Under my breath I added, "Besides, you can't go. I'm not wed yet. We have a bargain."

Chapter Four

After dinner that night I returned to Trina's chamber, but she was asleep, and Milton wouldn't let me wake her. Then, before I awoke the next morning, a carriage took her away from Bamarre castle.

I thought of her often in the weeks that followed. I decided that she must be defying the Gray Death. She might hesitate at first, but as she weakened, she would become frightened and then she'd begin to struggle. I imagined her forcing herself to stand and then to walk, then to go outdoors. I imagined her reveling in her restored health.

I thought of Rhys often too. He kept his promise, and I saw no more spiders. I was grateful every time I stepped briskly into a room or walked confidently down a corridor. I told Meryl about the spiders' banishment, and she rejoiced with me, but she had little interest in Rhys since he didn't ride a horse or wield a sword.

I wondered how he had accomplished the spider miracle and the cloud trick. I knew little about sorcerers, although I knew about the spectacle of their birth. They were born when lightning struck marble, which happens rarely enough. They had no parents and no brothers or sisters.

People wealthy enough to own marble put a slab of it outdoors during storms in hopes of witnessing a birth. Father always did so, but we'd never been lucky.

When a birth occurred, the lightning and the marble begot a flame that grew and unfolded as might a quick-blooming rose. Within the flame would be the sorcerer—full grown, still glowing, his nakedness covered by a shimmering cocoon.

He would look about him for a moment. Then he would look inward and learn what he was. In a burst of joy he would rocket into the sky, into the storm, showering sparks. The speed of his flight would burn off his cocoon, but a spark of the flame that gave him life would burn on in his chest, sustaining him until death.

This was all I knew. To learn more, I went to the library and looked sorcerers up in *The*

Book of Beings. After the description of their birth, I read:

LIFE SPAN: Sorcerers need only air to live. They may eat and drink for pleasure, but they need not. They are incapable of sleep. Although they never take ill, they may die in as many other ways as humans can, by accident or by design or in war. If they do not meet with disaster, however, then at the end of five hundred years their spark is extinguished, and they die.

During their first two hundred years they are apprentices, and they live out in the world. At the end of that time, they are journeymen and retreat to their citadel, which they rarely leave again.

APPEARANCE: Their most distinguishing feature is their white eyelashes. All sorcerers, whether male or female, young or old, have dark wavy hair. The species runs to tallness: The average height of a female is five feet and ten inches; the average height of a male is six feet and two inches. All have long, tapering fingers and long, graceful necks. The faces are individual, with as much variety of feature as is seen in humankind. Immature sorcerers have the open, unlined faces of youth.

DISPOSITION AND RELATIONS WITH HUMANS: Sorcerers are neither universally good nor universally bad. There have been heroes and villains, but most sorcerers, like most humans, are a blend of good and bad qualities.

Although most are indifferent to humans, some of the young go through a phase of intense interest that always terminates at the end of their apprenticeship. Sorcerers rarely marry, and they never marry each other. A few marriages between sorcerers and humans have occurred, and children have been born of such unions.

The section ended, and I slammed the book shut. It hadn't told me what magic the sorcerers could do, what went on at their citadel, or even how many sorcerers there were.

Rhys and I did speak again, but not often. Father kept sending him off to distant regions, to help farmers with the weather and to report on monster depredations.

I met Rhys a few times by accident in the

castle corridors. Each time, he stopped to talk. Once he told me of a fair in Dettford where a performer had danced a jig on the heads of ten villagers, who could hardly stand still for laughing. Another time he described a tapestry in an earl's castle that illustrated the meeting between Willard, an early Bamarrian king, and the specter that had predicted the cure to the Gray Death. He added that the tapestry was *almost* as skillfully done as my embroideries.

But he never sought me out. I saw him most often during dinner in the banquet hall. Indeed, in his peacock's attire, he was hard to miss.

He was very different from me. He was dramatic. He smiled easily, frowned easily, and laughed easily and with abandon, head thrown back, shoulders heaving.

Once I saw him fly. I had been sitting in my window seat, sketching. It was a gray day, and a fine mist was falling.

He stood with Father in the courtyard. Father read something from *The Book of Homely Truths*, the book of sayings he quoted constantly. Then he closed the book and raised his hand in a gesture of parting. Rhys lifted effortlessly, as smoke rises. From a few feet up he bowed to Father. Then he sailed off—backward. I was beginning to know him, and I suspected that he was showing off. I wondered if he knew I was watching.

Before I met Rhys, I'd been infatuated with Drualt for years. I used to put myself to sleep at night by imagining meetings with him. I'd tell him my long catalogue of fears, and he'd comfort me and describe his adventures.

But now I imagined meetings with Rhys instead. I wouldn't mention my fears, because I wanted him to think well of me. In their place I told him about my sketches and my embroidery designs, and he told me about his experiences in Bamarre. At some point he always mentioned that he adored talking to me, and I always blushed and mumbled that I liked talking to him too.

I'd never before been infatuated with someone living, someone real. However, infatuation with Rhys was as foolish as infatuation with a legendary hero. I was still a child, and Rhys was a sorcerer.

When I was sixteen, Father began building a new wing to Bamarre castle. Rhys was needed to straighten walls and to keep stones from falling on the laborers.

The sitting room that had been our nursery overlooked the work. Whenever I had time, I'd sit there with my embroidery and watch. Once

Rhys saw me and waved.

Then, after a week, he took pains to find me—and Meryl and Bella too. He stationed himself in the garden, along the route we took on our afternoon walk.

The irises were in bloom, and I had been thinking of sketching them when we turned into the rose walk. There was Rhys, seated on a bench, head tilted back, breathing in the perfumed air so deeply that I could see his chest rise and fall.

He sprang up, and I felt Bella stiffen. She considered sorcerers to be outsiders, and she distrusted them.

When we got near, he bowed. "Princesses, Mistress Bella." That day his doublet had green-and-blue stripes, and his boots sported golden spurs.

The three of us curtsied.

"I have gifts for you, if I may." He picked something up from the bench, a sword in a silver scabbard. He knelt to present it to Meryl. "I believe you like to fence, Your Highness."

She took the sword and drew it out of the scabbard. "It's beautiful." She held it out for me to see. "Isn't it splendid?"

It was, but I hated it. She had no need for a sword, not while I was still unwed.

She must have seen something in my expression, because she touched my shoulder and said in a low voice, "Stop worrying, Addie." Then she began to fence with a rosebush. "Take that, you dastardly roses. Take that." She parried and thrust, handling the sword easily, as graceful as a festival dancer.

"Meryl, a princess doesn't—" Bella began.

"See how it catches the sunlight? Sword, I dub you Blood-biter." Blood-biter was Drualt's sword. "I've longed for a sword, but . . ." She looked up at Rhys. "How did you know?"

He smiled. "You've been seen practicing with a wooden training sword."

"Thank you. I'll use it well."

Don't use it at all!

"I have something for you too, Mistress Bella." Rhys reached into the pouch at his waist.

"I can't accept a . . ."

Her voice tapered off as Rhys drew out an object I'd never seen before. Meryl stopped fencing and came close to see.

It was the size of my hand, pearly white with tints of rose and blue, wide at one end, coming to a point at the other.

"Is it?" Bella breathed.

"Yes. It's a scale from a dragon's tail."

Bella reached for it.

"Take care. The tip is very sharp."

"Did you slay the dragon?" Meryl asked in a hushed, reverent tone.

Bella took the scale by the wide end. "Thank you, Rhys." She curtsied.

He bowed yet again. "No, I didn't slay the dragon. The scale comes from our sorcerers' citadel, where there are many wondrous things."

I hoped he had something for me too. "Can I touch it?" I asked.

Bella held it out. It felt warm, and so dry it seemed to draw moisture from my finger.

"Does it have any power?" Meryl said.

Bella opened her mouth to answer, but Rhys spoke first. "It's versatile, Princess Meryl. Hold it in your hand, and you'll be cozy warm on the coldest day. Place it on your mantel, and mice and rats will stay away from your hearth. Boil it in a pot, and you'll have a tasty broth, fiery and a little bitter. Take it out of the pot, dry it off, and it makes a superior letter opener." He bowed yet again.

Bella placed the scale carefully in her reticule.

"And the best part," Meryl said, "is that the dragon who owned the scale is dead. That's the very best part." She started walking toward the castle, lunging and thrusting as she went.

We followed.

"Be careful," Bella called. She left my side and hurried to catch up to Meryl.

Rhys walked next to me. "I have a gift for you too, Princess Addie."

I shook my head, embarrassed about wishing for one.

He reached into a pocket in his doublet and held out a smooth wooden ball not much bigger than a walnut shell. I noticed a thin seam running along the middle. "This is more than it seems." He twisted the ball, and it opened along the seam.

Out came yards and yards of deep-blue cloth, amazingly fine to fit into such a small container. He held it out for me to touch. It was as soft as a kitten's breath.

"And there." He pointed.

Poking out of a corner of the cloth was the thinnest needle I'd ever seen.

I looked up at him. He was smiling, and when I met his eyes, his smile widened. He looked utterly pleased, as if *I* had given *him* a present. He wound the cloth around his finger and placed it back in the wooden ball. "Here."

I took it, already thinking of what I could

embroider on it. A moonlit forest scene . . . Drualt with a specter . . .

"Thank you." That wasn't enough. "I'll try to add to its beauty." Then, without thinking, I reached up and touched his cheek. I felt his warm skin and pulled my hand away.

Bella called me. "Come, Addie."

"I must go." I ran to her, sorry to leave and glad to get away.

Chapter Five

*I*n our sitting room I showed the gift to Meryl and Bella.

"I like Rhys," Meryl said. "He's the best sorcerer Father's ever had."

"I like him too," I murmured.

"We should give him gifts in return," she added.

Bella agreed. "It's only polite. I'll pick out one of my doilies."

I was delighted. "Maybe he'd like that cushion cover I finished last week," I said. "Do you think sorcerers use cushions?"

"What could I give him?" Meryl's stitchery was more tangle than stitch.

"You could declaim for him," I said. Her recitations were masterful. When she declaimed in our sitting room, the couch cushions fluffed up, the chairs straightened their backs, and the table stood an inch taller.

Meryl spoke to Rhys in the banquet hall that evening. They agreed to meet three days hence, which would be Thursday. I could hardly wait.

I wanted Rhys to become better acquainted with Meryl and for the three of us to be friends.

On Tuesday Bella had one of her headaches and couldn't give us our lesson. Meryl seized the opportunity and persuaded me to ride with her to Lake Orrinic.

I rarely ventured beyond the fields that bordered Bamarre castle, but the lake was only five miles away, and monsters had never come so close as that. I was eager to go because I wanted fresh views for my embroidery, and Lake Orrinic bordered a pine forest and a cliff.

The day was sunny and hot. We spread our blanket on the lakeshore.

"I'm off to explore." Meryl pointed at a cave in the cliff and brandished Blood-biter. "Perhaps the bats know how to fence."

After she'd gone, I began to sketch an episode from *Drualt*. In my drawing Drualt stood on a rock in the middle of Lake Orrinic, battling a flock of gryphons. The air was full of feathers, and Drualt laughed as he fought. One of the gryphons had a hurt wing, and a wound over its eye dripped blood.

Sometimes my images of gore and mayhem made even Meryl uneasy, but they never troubled me. A real monster battle would have caused me to die of terror, but a painted or stitched one gave me only pleasure.

I forgot everything while I drew, but after I finished, I began to worry about Meryl. She should have come out of the cave by now. I ran to its mouth and called into it. My only answer was a ripple of echoes. As I took a few steps inside, I made out the bones of a dead squirrel in the shadows a few feet away.

A passageway led deeper into the cave. I hoped Meryl hadn't gone exploring in there. I called to her again. The echoes sounded despairing. I backed out, telling myself that she had probably left the cave anyway.

I hurried to the pine forest, the only other place she might be. The trees were huge, some taller than our castle battlements. I stood at the forest's edge, peering in and feeling as tiny as a mole. I saw no movement and heard nothing. The silence frightened me. It seemed to be holding its breath, waiting.

Meryl is fine, I told myself. I started back to the lake, wondering if I should gallop home and return with guards to search the cave and the forest.

"Lady!"

I turned. A child stepped out of the shadows several yards into the woods.

"Lady!" He ran to me and bowed clumsily.

He was about six years old, in torn breeches and a dirty shirt. He was a comely child, with a sweet plump face. His hair was amber ringlets, mussed on top, as if he'd been caught in brambles. I wondered what he'd been doing in the forest. Perhaps his father was a woodcutter.

"Are you the other princess? Princess . . ." He shook his head. "I forgot."

My heart started pounding. "Have you seen my sister?"

"What's your name? She made me promise—"

"I'm Princess Adelina, Addie. Now tell me."

He dimpled when he smiled. "That's the one. She said—"

"Tell me! Is she all right?"

He nodded. "She wants you to come. She found something. She said you have to see it."

Thank heaven she was all right. "What is it?"

He dimpled again. "I mustn't say."

My fear of the forest receded. Meryl would never send for me if there was danger. I was so glad to know where she was!

He held his hand out to me, and I took it. It was moist and surprisingly cool, considering how warm the day was.

He began to talk, while holding my hand

confidingly. I smiled down at him. He'd seen Meryl doing something, he wouldn't say what, and she'd paid him to find me. He opened his other hand and showed me a silver coin. "I'm going to buy gingerbread."

He led me a few steps into the forest. The pine needles underfoot made a soft carpet.

I stopped short. There could be spiders.

The boy looked up at me curiously.

Meryl wouldn't have sent for me if there were spiders. She wouldn't forget.

"How far is she?"

"Not far. Perhaps a quarter—"

A stone caught him behind the ear, and I saw blood. We both spun around.

Meryl was running toward us from the direction of the cave.

Meryl! But she was in the forest. How could she be here?

She stopped every few steps to pick up a fresh stone and throw it. In her left hand she waved Blood-biter.

A stone gashed the child's forehead, and more blood flowed. He began to cry.

"Meryl! What are you doing? Stop!" With my free hand I found my handkerchief and pressed it to his forehead.

"Let go of him, Addie!"

He was only a child! But I dropped his hand.

Meryl reached us and pointed her sword at the child.

His wails rose in pitch. I wanted to hug him and comfort him. What was Meryl doing?

"Get away from my sister! You can't have her!"

He stopped crying and began to giggle mischievously. Then he changed, thinned. I could see the trees through his open, laughing mouth.

He—it—was a specter! I stepped back, stunned.

It was vanishing.

"Stop, monster!" Meryl said. "I command you."

Its face filled in again, but its body remained wraithlike, transparent. A monster, there in front of me!

"Do you think me a child?" Meryl asked. "I found you out, and now you must prophesy for me. When will my adventures begin?"

It continued to giggle, and now I saw its malice. "You've just had your first adventure, so they've already begun. But your next one will not be what you expect." It laughed harder and began to vanish again.

"When will that be?"

"Only one question." A last shriek of laughter, and it disappeared.

"Oh, Meryl!" I would have gone with it. It would have gotten me hopelessly lost. I would have wandered until I died of starvation or despair. "How did you know?"

"I didn't know, but I guessed. It was too beautiful, and I wondered how it got here."

In spite of my fright, I wanted to cry over the loss of such a sweet lad. It would have killed me, and I was sad over losing it. That was power. I couldn't stop trembling.

Meryl crouched down. "See, Addie? It left no footprints. That's how you can tell a specter."

I looked. The ground on the edge of the forest was soft and moist. There were half a dozen impressions of my boots and Meryl's but none of the boy's. The specter's.

She stood up. "What do you think it meant about my next adventure?"

I shook my head and continued to tremble. It had meant something horrible, I was sure.

"It could have told me when," Meryl grumbled. "That wasn't really a separate question."

"You know when," I whispered. "After I'm wed."

Then I swore to myself that I'd never marry. Bamarre would be too perilous without Meryl.

Chapter Six

I was weepy and trembly for the rest of the day. It was fortunate that specters never came indoors, or I would have suspected every elf and servant I didn't know well.

I wouldn't let Meryl out of my sight, and by nightfall she was impatient with me. We were in our sitting room, and she was trying to develop a battle plan for a company of forty knights against a pack of seven ogres. I had Rhys's cloth in my lap and was absently stroking it.

"Addie! Stop worrying. I can't concentrate."

"I'm not doing anything."

"Every minute or so you shudder, and then you glance at me."

Just seeing her reassured me. I faced her profile, her stubborn, square jaw, and her snub nose. She was hunched over our small table, and her toe tapped a rhythm on the braided rug. An oil lamp was at her elbow, and I made out an ink stain on her knuckle and one on her sleeve.

"I have to work this out. Listen, Addie." She

looked up. "If the terrain is rough and the ogres are throwing rocks, what should the knights do in defense?"

"Gallop away?"

"I should have known better than to ask you." She bent over her notebook again.

By Thursday my fright had receded, dispatched by my excitement over giving Rhys his gift. My only worry was that it might rain. But it didn't, although the day stayed cloudy.

When we arrived in the garden, he was already there. I put his cushion behind my back so he wouldn't see.

He ran to us, then bowed. "Princesses, Mistress Bella, I'm so—"

"We have gifts for you, Rhys," Meryl said, curtsying.

He fell back a step. "I want no—"

"There may be a law against refusing a royal gift," Meryl said.

He looked surprised. "I wasn't . . ." He bowed again. "I shall be honored to accept your gifts."

"You first, Bella," Meryl said.

She handed Rhys his doily and stood stiffly, waiting.

He held the doily in open palms. "It's so intricate."

She smiled smugly.

"I will treasure it, Mistress Bella." He folded it carefully and put it into the pouch at his waist.

I held my gift out. I'd never felt more shy. "I hope you like it."

He looked at the cushion. "It's a scene from *Drualt*, isn't it? He's so much smaller than the ogres, yet I can see he's going to vanquish them. It's his posture, his confidence." He looked up. "How did you manage that?"

I shrugged, not sure how to answer.

"And that ogre's expression!" Rhys laughed. "Stupid and angry and sly, all at once. You're a sorcerer with thread, Princess Addie."

"It *is* magic," Meryl agreed.

"Her Highness is an accomplished needle-woman," Bella said primly.

They all smiled at me.

"It's Meryl's turn," I said, uncomfortable with the attention.

"Not here," she said. We were on the garden's busiest path. "Let's go to the old court-yard."

I nodded. No one would bother us there.

Meryl led the way, speaking over her shoulder. "I am going to declaim for you. I'm very good at it."

"She's wonderful," I murmured.

The old courtyard was on the northern side of the castle, ringed by grapevines. Grass grew between the cracked paving stones, and the fountain no longer spouted. The wooden bench had once been painted, but now it was gray.

Meryl stationed herself in front of the fountain. Rhys motioned me onto the bench. Bella sat next to me, and he stood on my other side. I felt him there the whole time Meryl spoke.

"I will recite Drualt's battle with the dragon Yune. First we are introduced to the dragon and then to Drualt, although we have met the hero before." She took a deep breath and began.

> *"Fiery breath,*
> *Snapping teeth, volcanic spittle;*
> *Soft underbelly*
> *Ringed by living spikes,*
> *Poison tipped.*
> *Patient and relentless*
> *As the desert sand,*
> *Dealing hot death*
> *In bitter morsels—*
> *The dragon Yune."*

Meryl was a master at the traditional intonations and gestures of Bamarrian recitation.

Her voice snapped along with the dragon's teeth and whipped along with her tail. In truth she almost became the dragon. When she mentioned Yune's underbelly, she even stuck out her own stomach and rubbed it.

"Now the poem speaks of Drualt.

> *"No scales, no whipping tail,*
> *Only a shining face,*
> *Beacon in battle.*
> *Only a man, the laugher,*
> *Tall among men,*
> *The warrior Drualt.*

"Back to the dragon.

> *"Yune's hoard—*
> *Knights' bones,*
> *Gnawed white;*
> *Maidens' bones,*
> *Charred black;*
> *Ruby brooch;*
> *Tiara of diamonds;*
> *My lady's golden slipper—*
> *Yune's hoard,*
> *Tall as a tower.*

"Drualt once again.

> "Drualt's army—
> Defiance, Drualt's steed.
> Gore-gouger, Drualt's dagger;
> Blood-biter, Drualt's sword;
> Drualt's own sturdy legs,
> Mainstay and Helpmeet;
> Drualt's own mighty arms,
> Defender and Thruster.
> Drualt's army,
> Sinew and steel."

Meryl's delivery was riveting. She had never been better. The introduction went on for a few more minutes, followed by Drualt's challenge and Yune's taunting reply. Then hero and monster battled in the empty desert outside Yune's cave.

> "Yune exhaled a cloud
> Of vapors hot and thick,
> Bitter as bile.
> The cloud engulfed
> Drualt's army.
> Within the cloud,
> Defiance stumbled,
> Choking.

Hooves beat the smoke.
Drualt, the laugher,
Heard Yune's laugh.
He raised Blood-biter, and,
Glowing white, the sword carved
A tunnel, a sun shaft
To pure air
And, unseen,
To Yune."

Next to me, Bella mouthed the words as Meryl spoke them. I glanced up at Rhys. He leaned forward, intent, nodding as Meryl spoke.

She kept reciting. Drualt used the cloud as cover to get under Yune's wing. He stabbed at her underbelly, wounding her. They battled for hours, and each was wounded several times. Then the tide turned against Drualt. He was unhorsed, and Blood-biter was knocked out of his hand. Before he could reclaim the sword, Yune's flame melted it.

Meryl looked pale, and I thought I saw a tremor run through her. This is exhausting her, I thought, and wondered why. But her voice was steady, deeper and richer than usual.

Drualt knew that cunning alone would save

him. He raced to Yune's hoard, fire licking his heels, and dove into it. Yune swallowed her flame, not wanting to harm her treasure. She pawed the pile of bones and jewels, searching for Drualt.

> *"Within the moldering,*
> *Noxious hoard,*
> *Drualt's living hand*
> *Found the sword*
> *Of long-dead hero*
> *Arkule. Yune's claws*
> *Raked her festering pile*
> *And almost plucked out Drualt's*
> *Keen right eye.*
> *A claw found instead*
> *Drualt's scorched shoulder.*
> *The dragon shrieked her triumph:*
> *'You're mine now. Mine!*
> *Mine to burn, mine to crisp,*
> *Mine to kill.'*
> *She lifted Drualt.*
> *And on that upward journey*
> *To his doom,*
> *Drualt thrust Gore-gouger*
> *Into Yune's soft flesh*
> *And plunged—"*

Meryl broke off, panting and holding her side. Bella and I jumped up. Rhys took a step toward her.

She held up her hand. "I'm fine.

> *". . . plunged Arkule's long*
> *And ancient sword*
> *Into Yune's stony heart."*

The recitation was over. Meryl began to curtsy, lost her balance, and almost fell. Then she caught herself and completed the obeisance. She stood and smiled.

The smile was forced, I thought, too brilliant to be real.

Rhys applauded wildly, flamboyantly. I stood and clapped. Bella clapped too, but she was frowning. She and I knew that Meryl usually went on reciting to the end of the dragon stanzas, through Yune's collapse, Drualt's narrow escape from suffocation, and the reunion with his horse, Defiance. She always insisted that the battle wasn't properly over until every uncertainty had been resolved.

"Wonderful! Marvelous!" Rhys was still clapping. "I've never heard it done so well."

"Thank you." Meryl sank onto the bench.

Rhys's expression changed from delight to worry.

She must have caught a cold, I thought, sitting next to her.

"You should rest in your room," Bella said. "Such a warm day . . . the exertion . . ."

"I'm not tired. Reciting always gives me energy. You know that."

But she continued to sit. Ordinarily, after declaiming, she could almost leap tall trees.

"Now it's my turn to entertain." Rhys still looked worried. "Apprentices aren't supposed to, but . . ." He smiled ruefully. "I can't resist."

He took Meryl's place at the fountain. "I can use those clouds." He took out his golden baton and pointed it upward. . . .

And we were in a fog so thick that when I looked down, my arms faded into it above the elbow.

I heard Rhys say, "No. No."

The fog vanished, and a compact little cloud floated above the fountain. A roll of thunder came from the cloud—lighter and sweeter than ordinary thunder. It was little-cloud thunder, without lightning but with rhythm, ta-dum *dum*, ta-dum *dum*. The cloud pulsed in time to itself, a dancing cloud.

I smiled. Meryl was smiling too, leaning against my shoulder. I looked up at Bella, whose face was impassive. She wasn't to be won over so easily.

Rhys raised his baton again. A wisp of cloud came to hang in the air next to its thundering cousin. Rhys pointed his baton at the wispy cloud, and it began to wave as if in a stiff wind. We heard the wind, first loud *SHHH*, then soft *shhh*, loud *SHHH*, soft *shhh*.

Ta-dum *dum SHHH*, ta-dum *dum shhh*, ta-dum *dum SHHH*.

Now Rhys returned to the little cloud with his baton, and the little cloud started to rain. The raindrops hit the paving stones with high metallic taps and low slurpy plops and sharp plinks and soft thuds, making music, merry silly gurgling music.

Meryl and I were laughing, and even Bella was smiling. I found myself bobbing in time to the clouds, and Meryl was conducting with her finger.

Then Rhys began to sing, compounding the silliness, his voice sliding all over the scale, high falsetto one moment, bass the next. "Thank you for my presents," he sang. "Thank you, Princess Meryl, for declaiming, and thank you, Mistress Bella, for my doily, and thank you, Princess Addie, for my cushion. Thank you for being my new friends."

He raised his baton, and the music came to a wild crescendo. Then, with a wave, he sent the clouds back to the sky. He bowed.

We applauded, and I clapped until my palms tingled. I expected Meryl to heap praise on him, but she was silent. So I said, "That was enchanting, wasn't it, Meryl?"

She nodded, smiling. Then she stood. "I'm tired. Bella, I'd like to—"

"Excuse us, Rhys." Bella leaped up. She put an arm around Meryl's shoulder. "She must be getting a cold. Rest will be the cure."

"Thank you for the entertainment," Meryl said. She curtsied and turned to leave.

I turned too.

"Wait, Princess Addie," Rhys said. "Can you stay a moment longer?"

I blushed and nodded, feeling glad, wondering what he'd say.

They left, but he didn't speak. He just stared after them. When they disappeared around the grape vines, he faced me, and there were tears in his eyes.

"Some of you die so young." He looked up at the sky. "I talked about it with Orne, my teacher, but he only said, 'They live briefly. That is their lot.'" Rhys shook his head. "He has no sympathy. Your sister . . ." He stopped again. "Oh, Princess Addie. I hate to say—"

"What?" My voice rose. "What?"

"It began today. She didn't have it yesterday. It happens that way. Princess Meryl . . . has the Gray Death."

Chapter Seven

"Meryl?" I forced a laugh. "This morning she ran from her chamber to the stable, and then we rode for an hour."

"I've seen it too often. I lived in a village . . ."

Meryl have the Gray Death? She couldn't. Not Meryl.

"It's impossible," I said calmly. "You don't know her. Meryl is the last person who'd get it. She's too strong. She'd refuse to get it." My voice rose. "And how would you know? You're not an elf. You're not even—"

"I've seen hundreds sick with it." He took my hands.

I pulled them away. "She isn't sick. You'll see." I ran to the castle. She couldn't be sick. I'd find Milton. He'd tell me she was fine.

Milton wasn't in the apothecary. Two elves I hardly knew were there. I heard Meryl's name, but that meant nothing. I wheeled and ran.

Bella stood in the hall outside Meryl's chamber, weeping. I dashed by her and opened the door.

Meryl was in a nightdress, sitting up in bed, Blood-biter in her lap. My heart lifted when I saw her. She looked like herself. She was Meryl—only in bed in the middle of the afternoon.

Milton was arranging anemones in a vase on the table next to the bed. Anemones! Flowers of the dying. I flew at him and pulled them out of his hand.

"She doesn't need these!" I ran to a window, cranked it open, and threw them out.

"Milton says I have the Gray Death."

I turned around. I saw how afraid she was. Her eyes were huge. But she was never afraid.

I ran to her. "Milton's wrong." I glared at him. "You're frightening her." He wasn't frightening me. She didn't have it.

He met my eyes, and his were the saddest I'd ever seen.

I sat on the bed and hugged her hard.

"Blood-biter feels so heavy, Addie." She turned it over in her lap.

It couldn't! "You're tired. That's all. Does anything hurt?"

She shook her head. "When Milton said I had the Gray Death, I didn't believe him either. I went to Blood-biter to prove him wrong. I wanted to show him my swordplay. But I could barely take Blood-biter down from the mantelpiece." She choked out a laugh. "How will I slay monsters and save Bamarre if I can't lift my sword?"

"You'll slay monsters," I said. "You'll slay a hundred monsters. If it *is* the Gray Death, you can battle it and win."

She laughed again—half sob, half laugh. "I'm not supposed to be the one who gets sick. I'm supposed to find the cure."

"If you fight the disease and win, you will have found the cure," I said.

How could she be so sick? I watched her face. I couldn't tell what she was thinking. Generally I knew, but now I didn't.

She couldn't have the Gray Death.

A warm breeze wafted in from the open window and, along with it, the shouts of the servants' children playing in the garden.

Meryl said, "Addie, this morning in the stable, before you came down, I spoke sharply to one of the grooms. He was only dawdling a little. You would never have scolded. If I had been kinder . . ." She stopped and then went on. "If I had been kinder, do you think the Gray Death would have left me alone?"

I shook my head, unable to speak. Finally I said, "It's not your fault you're sick." I repeated,

"It's not your fault, and you don't have it."

Father and Rhys came in, followed by Bella. I curtsied. Milton bowed.

"Good afternoon, Father," Meryl said.

He advanced to the bed in his usual stately way, his expression as serene as ever.

That meant it couldn't be true. If it were true, he'd be rushing to her. He'd be distressed. Even he would be.

"Daughter . . . Meryl." He turned to Milton. "Are you sure she's ill?"

"Yes, Sire. It's the Gray Death."

Father pulled a small worn book from the pocket of his mantle. It was his constant companion, his beloved advisor.

He said, "I consulted *The Book of Homely Truths*." He opened it and read, "'Half measures will not root out a canker.' In the past I've sent emissaries to search for the cure to the Gray Death. *Homely Truths* tells me that this is not enough. I must go myself."

I wasn't sure I'd heard right. Father had never dared go far from Bamarre castle.

"Daughter . . ."

"Yes, Father?"

He put out his hand to touch her but then withdrew it. "Farewell. I'll leave in the morning. Come, Rhys." He started for the door.

Rhys looked at Meryl and then at me. He bowed and followed Father.

As soon as the door closed, Bella hurried to Meryl. "Slide under the covers! You'll get chilled."

She was trying to treat the Gray Death as if it were a cold. That brought my tears, and with them, belief. Meryl had the Gray Death. I ran out of the room.

In the corridor the flood came. I went into my chamber next door and threw myself on the bed, sobbing.

I saw a thousand images of Meryl—Meryl practicing her swordplay, Meryl galloping on Bane, Meryl poring over her battle strategy books, Meryl listening to my worries, Meryl comforting me, Meryl telling me stories, Meryl saving me from a specter. Meryl strong, Meryl cocky, Meryl brave. *Meryl.*

I wept and wept, but then I made myself stop. I forced myself to swallow my tears and made myself breathe slowly, deeply. I would not cry over her as though she were already dead when she wasn't going to die at all.

She would fight the Gray Death and win.

Or Father would find the cure.

I remembered the ancient prophecy: The Gray Death would be cured when cowards found courage and rain fell over all Bamarre. Father seemed to have found courage, so perhaps the other part would come true too.

There was hope. The clouds hadn't cleared since Meryl declaimed. Clouds might be gathering everywhere in Bamarre. Rain might be on the way.

And Meryl was so strong and lively. Why couldn't she defeat the Gray Death?

I wondered what had happened to Trina, although it didn't matter. Trina was no Meryl.

I laughed bitterly. I'd spent years worrying that Meryl would leave Bamarre castle and be killed. I'd never thought she could stay home and be killed.

Chapter Eight

I didn't sleep that night. I listened for rain, and I cried again and couldn't stop myself.

Eventually dawn came. No rain, but the skies were still cloudy.

I dressed and hurried downstairs to see Father off. But in the courtyard I found only a yawning lad with a broom. He informed me that King Lionel had just sat down to his breakfast.

Why did he tarry? Meryl couldn't wait. I rushed to the banquet hall and hovered in the doorway. Father was there, chewing slowly, nodding slowly at something the councillor at his left was saying.

I wheeled and ran to the stables. Grooms dashed here and there. One was saddling Father's charger. Several knights were seeing to their own horses, instructing their squires.

Somewhat reassured, I returned to the castle. Meryl was still asleep, although she never slept past seven and it was now almost eight. Milton was in a blue chair, knitting. He nodded at me when I came in. I sat down in the window seat.

Every few minutes I looked down at the courtyard to see if Father had come out. I began to wonder if he'd changed his mind.

At nine thirty Meryl opened her eyes. She smiled at me, and then I watched her remember that she was sick. She stopped smiling and squeezed her eyes shut. She opened them again in a wide-eyed stare, her angry expression. I'd seen her look this way a thousand times, at bad news about monsters, at Bella's silliest rules, at Father's cowardice. Never at me.

I stood to go to her, but she shook her head.

"Leave me alone, Addie."

I sat down again.

"No, I mean go away. Milton can stay with me."

Why was she angry at me? I started for the door.

"Addie?"

I turned, hope rising.

"Milton will find you when you can come back."

I went to my room, my dismissal an added misery. I looked out the window, but the courtyard was empty. I thought repeatedly about barging in on Meryl and refusing to leave.

At last, shortly before noon, Father and his knights began to gather. I ran downstairs, relieved to be doing something.

I was surprised Father was taking only fifteen knights. There should be a battalion at least. No, the entire army should march out to save Meryl, every knight, every archer, every pikeman.

The knights made a busy, noisy scene—armor clanking, horses stamping and snorting. In the midst of it all Father sat calmly on his horse, gazing at the land beyond our drawbridge. He was in full armor, although his helmet was in his lap.

Go, I thought. Leave. You've wasted enough time.

A small crowd had gathered. Rhys was there, standing near a knot of Father's councillors. I went to him, and, as always, he bowed.

I curtsied and then spoke softly so only he would hear. "Do you know where Father plans to go?"

"I heard him say he would go first to the elf queen, since she knows the remedy for many ailments."

But that made no sense. If Queen Seema had known the cure to the Gray Death, she would have told her elf nurses about it. What's more, the high road east to her castle was the best and safest in Bamarre. Father had found courage in a small way, if he had found it at all.

He saw me and gestured for me to approach. I did, dodging a prancing stallion on my way.

"Good-bye, Daughter. As *The Book of Homely Truths* tells us, 'Departure is a new beginning for those who depart and for those who remain behind.' May it be so."

"Farewell, Father. May success ride with you." Save Meryl. Save me.

He pulled on his helmet and spurred his horse. His knights fell into place behind him. They were off. I looked up at the sky, hoping the clouds were thickening.

When Father and his knights had crossed the drawbridge, I turned back to the castle, Rhys at my side. I'd been away from Meryl for hours. Surely she'd let me in now.

Rhys said nothing, but I felt his sadness.

"Meryl is going to be fine," I said. "She'll get her strength back, or Father will find the cure."

Rhys was still silent.

I stopped walking. "Can't you do something for her? You're a sorcerer."

"Oh, Princess Addie."

"Isn't there some magic to make her

stronger or to make the Gray Death weaker?"

He kept shaking his head. He looked like a fool, wagging his head. What were sorcerers good for? I started walking again, faster.

"We don't have enough power. Only fairies do," he said, keeping up with me easily.

"I know," I murmured, sorry for making him feel bad.

Neither of us spoke for a minute. Then he said, "King Lionel has instructed me to fly to him every day until I have to go to our citadel." He added, "There's a ceremony for the apprentices. I wish it weren't taking place so soon."

"When will you leave?"

"In a week. I'll be gone nine days." He held the wooden door to the stairway open for me. "Until then, the king will let me know his progress every day, and I'm to advise his council." He paused.

I looked up.

He was blushing. "And you too."

His blush gave him away. Father would never remember me unless *Homely Truths* told him to.

Without thinking I asked, "Must you go to your citadel?"

"Yes. I must."

"Can't you arrive late?" I was begging. It was

shameful, but with Meryl sick and shutting me out, I needed someone to . . . protect me? Tears pricked my eyelids again. I was such a coward. Like Father.

Rhys said, "I can't arrive late. I'll be drawn there whether or not I want to go."

"Oh."

We walked the rest of the way in silence. I wondered if Meryl was still angry at me.

When we reached her chamber, I paused. What if she still didn't want me? I knocked.

"Come in." Her voice sounded gay.

I saw Bella first, seated in a red chair by the fireplace. Then I saw Meryl. She was up and dressed, standing at the foot of her bed. Milton, holding Blood-biter, stood a few feet from her. Meryl opened her arms to me, and I ran into them.

She whispered into my neck, "I'm sorry, Addie. I was too angry to be with anyone healthy. I won't send you away again. Besides, I won't be sick for long." She tilted her head back. "I realized something."

I looked down at her.

Her eyes were shining. "It's what the specter meant. This is my next adventure! The Gray Death. You see, if it's an adventure, it can't be inevitable that I die."

Could she be right? I smiled back at her, nodding. Of course she was right!

"Now stand back and watch. Milton, give me my sword." She took it from him and raised it with both hands. Her arms shook from the effort. She lunged, lost her balance, and came down hard on one knee. Blood-biter clattered on the tiled floor.

We all rushed toward her.

"No!" She waved us away. "I will stand up on my own." She heaved herself up and stood still, panting. "See, Sir Gray Death. I can do what I want."

But she couldn't. She could hardly do anything.

Bella was weeping. I was horrified. Meryl was losing strength so quickly! If she continued this way, the next phase, the sleep, would come soon. After that she would have only twelve days left.

Rhys picked up the sword and gave it to her.

"Thank you." Using both hands, she lunged, and this time she didn't fall.

That was something.

"There," I said. "You did it."

"Put it away, please." She held the sword out to Rhys, her arms trembling again. "I'll practice more later. I think I'll walk now."

She headed for the door. She moved slowly but easily, I thought, till I saw her clenched fists and the vein throbbing in her forehead. At the door she turned and started toward the window.

The rest of us watched in strained silence.

By the fifth crossing she was breathing hard. She kept going for three more lengths, however. My legs ached and I gasped along with her. I had to bite my tongue to keep from begging her to rest.

She stopped. "Do you think that's enough, Addie? Rhys? Do you think I'm beating back Sir Gray Death?"

I was afraid she'd collapse, but I said, "I think Sir Gray Death hasn't met your like before."

Rhys agreed, and Milton helped her to bed.

"Bella, would you give us our lesson here today? I want it just as if— I want it. Tomorrow we'll be back in the library. Tomorrow—"

"You should rest," Bella said. "That's today's lesson—when people are sick, they rest."

"Addie thinks I shouldn't let Sir Gray Death gain sway over me."

"She can't give in," I agreed, hoping I was right. "I think we should have our lesson. Can you go over the end of *Drualt* and the monsters' assaults on Bamarre?" If anything could fortify Meryl against the Gray Death, that would.

Milton said a lesson would do no harm, so Bella called for servants to bring books and a table from the library. Rhys left us to go to the king's councillors.

The servants brought in three chairs and arranged them around the table. Meryl walked the two paces to the table in ten slow, small steps. She sat, breathing hard. I unclenched my hands and saw white nail marks on my palms.

Bella opened *Gryphons, Ogres, and Dragons: The Bamarrian Wars with Monsters*. She took her spectacles out of her reticule and assumed her governess voice. "I hope you remember that King Alfred was the first king whose records have come down to us." She began to read. "'When he had been king for three years, a tribe of ogres laid waste . . .'"

In the First Ogre War, it had taken King Alfred five years to drive a horde of ogres back to the Eskern Mountain Range, which formed our northern border. During the reign of Alfred's nephew, King Alfred II, the dragon Vollys began the raids on villages in the Bamarrian Plains that had gone on to this day.

When Bella paused, Meryl said, "Addie, do you remember what I said when Vollys carried off that farmer last year?"

I shook my head. I did remember, though. But I wouldn't have been able to say it without weeping.

"I said I'd slay Vollys someday and eat her eggs in an omelet." Meryl took a deep breath. "I'll still slay her. I hope you're listening, Sir Gray Death. I'll still do it."

"You'll do it!" I said, wanting to keep her spirits up. And my own.

"Meryl," Bella said, "a dragon would catch you as quick as look at you, illness or no. Vollys . . . Listen. It's in this very lesson." She began a long list of the dragon's depredations—farms burned, livestock eaten on the spot, families carried off, knights roasted in their armor, castles plundered. And all the humans—dead, or never seen again.

Bella passed on to the Second Ogre War. At first Meryl sat straight in her chair and asked questions or offered opinions. But after a quarter hour she became silent, and her hand came up to grip the tabletop.

She mustn't fall again! I stood. At the same moment Milton put down his knitting and went to her.

"You'll be no worse for resting," he said.

She nodded. "I think I'd be more comfortable in bed."

Bella closed her book.

"Don't stop the lesson." Meryl leaned on Milton's shoulder for the short trip to the bed.

I wondered if fighting the Gray Death was weakening her, or if she'd be even weaker if she weren't fighting.

Or if the Gray Death was in charge, and nothing else mattered.

Chapter Nine

"Say the end of *Drualt*, Bella," Meryl said as Milton tucked the blankets around her. "That will give me heart."

"Wouldn't you rather sleep a bit?"

Meryl shook her head emphatically.

She still has some energy, I thought desperately.

"I only hope you aren't sorry." Bella reached for the library's copy of *Drualt*. "You remember that Drualt is only nineteen when his story ends?"

Meryl and I nodded.

At this point in the epic, Drualt and his sweetheart, Freya, were battling the monsters alone. Earlier King Bruce's army and even ordinary Bamarrians had fought alongside them. Together they had beaten the monsters back to the mountains, the desert, and the forest. But as time passed, people became less willing to risk their lives against monsters that rarely troubled them.

Bella said, "The final episode begins when Drualt and his sweetheart pitch camp outside the walled village of Surmic, in the Eskern Mountains. Drualt goes hunting, and Freya sets off to fish in the Surmic River."

Meryl's eyes were closed, but she nodded as Bella spoke. Milton set down his knitting and listened.

Bella continued. "When the hero returns, he hears Freya crying for help. He gallops to the river, where he finds her harried by a dozen gryphons—and not a single villager has come to her defense.

"I will begin to read now.

> *"Two gryphons lay dead,*
> *Entrails spilling*
> *On the riverbank.*
> *Two gryphons staggered*
> *And reeled, wings savaged.*
> *Drualt laughed. His sweetheart*
> *Was a doughty warrior."*

Meryl opened her eyes and pushed herself higher in bed.

> *"Eight gryphons still*
> *Set upon Freya, feasting*

> *On her living flesh.*
> *Freya, down upon*
> *Her dimpled knees,*
> *Fought on, but*
> *Her life's blood poured*
> *Into the roiling river.*
> *Drualt's laughter died, and*
> *Nevermore did Drualt laugh*
> *Or smile in Bamarre."*

Bella's voice cracked, and she blew her nose into her handkerchief.

Meryl recited softly. But although her voice was weak, her delivery had as much feeling as ever.

> *"Though gryphons bit and clawed*
> *And set upon him, too,*
> *Drualt reached his sweetheart*
> *And knelt and tried*
> *To stanch the rush*
> *Of her heart's red blood."*

I began to cry. Today the loss of Freya was unbearable.

Bella took up the tale again. Drualt cradled Freya in his arms. He declared his love, and she spoke for the last time, saying she'd known he wouldn't desert her. Then she died.

Tears streamed down my face. Meryl was crying too. I ran to her and hugged her.

"I don't want to die," Meryl sobbed. "I don't want to die."

Bella flew to Meryl's other side. "Don't cry, sweet."

"Go on, Bella," Meryl gasped between sobs. "I want to hear it. . . . Just wait . . . a minute . . . It's doing . . . it will do me good."

We waited. I forgot my own tears as we all watched Meryl cry into my shoulder.

After a few minutes she pushed away from me. "I'm all right now. Crying is part of the adventure. Go on, Bella."

Bella took a moment to find her place. Then she began again.

> *"A monster pecked*
> *At Freya's dead lips.*
> *Drualt arose in fury and*
> *Slew it with one sweep*
> *Of his angry sword."*

Drualt killed the remaining gryphons quickly. When they lay dead, the gates of Surmic village

opened, and the villagers stepped out timidly.
Drualt shook his fist at them.

Bella recited, deepening her voice:

> *"'Come you now?' roared the hero.*
> *'Come you now, when all need*
> *Is past? Come you now,*
> *When my love is dead?'*
> *Frightened, the villagers*
> *Drew back and whispered*
> *Among themselves, their voices*
> *Dry as salt."*

Drualt lifted Freya and turned from the villagers. He began to walk away, bleeding from his many wounds. An old woman hurried and caught up to him. She asked if he would return to their aid in times of need.

> *"Drualt told the crone,*
> *'Bamarre will see no more of me*
> *Until the timid*
> *Go forth with the strong.*
> *But while her heroes*
> *Still fight alone,*
> *Bamarre will see no more of me.'"*

Meryl took my hands in hers, and I stroked her wrist with my thumb.

It was odd—I'd never before noticed the likeness between Drualt's vow and the specter's prediction of the Gray Death's cure. Drualt wouldn't return until the timid went forth with the strong, and the cure wouldn't be found until cowards found courage. I wished for meaning that could help Meryl, but I saw only coincidence. Still, it was curious.

Meryl began to murmur along with Bella.

> *"Drualt went then*
> *Into the mountains,*
> *Carrying Freya,*
> *Bold spirit, lost love.*
> *And he was no more*
> *Seen in Bamarre.*
>
> *"Now, when specter haunts,*
> *Or dragon flames,*
> *Or ogre attacks,*
> *Or gryphon descends,*
> *Bamarre fights alone.*
> *Drualt, the laugher,*
> *Tall among men,*
> *Is gone.*

But the tale has not
Run out—not yet.
So be brave, Bamarre!
Go forth, Bamarre,
The timid with the strong.
Let not your heroes
Fight alone.
Then one day,
In the spring of the year
When monsters are hunting,
A hero will come,
A laugher,
Tall among men.
Drualt, hero of Bamarre,
Will return.
So rise up, Bamarre!
Be brave, Bamarre!
Be worthy, Bamarre,
Of your hero's return."

Bella closed *Drualt*. Milton wiped his eyes. I would have wiped mine, except Meryl still held my hands, and I didn't want to pull away.

Chapter Ten

After the lesson Meryl fell asleep. I went to my bedchamber, where I slumped on my bed, too tired even to cry.

Too tired! That was how Meryl had felt after she declaimed. I leaped up, terrified.

I ran out into the corridor. I saw Milton in the distance, trundling away from me. I called out to him, and he waited.

"Yes, Princess Addie?"

The elves had seen Trina's stride and had known she was sick. Milton had watched me run to him, so he'd know by now.

"Milton . . ." I didn't know how to ask. "Er, I don't feel sick, but I'm so weary that I wondered . . . I wondered if—"

"You're not sick with the Gray Death," Milton said, smiling. "You're not a bit sick." When he smiled, his wrinkled cheeks became round as walnuts, and his eyes became slits of pleasure.

"Then why am I so tired?"

"Illness is exhausting, even when someone

else is ill." He reached up and touched my shoulder. "I often see this. People don't feel safe themselves when one they love is—"

"Meryl won't die." I turned and hurried away, almost as fast as I'd run toward him a minute before. When I turned into the next corridor, I slowed down, and then I wandered outside into the garden.

After a few minutes I found myself in the old courtyard where Meryl had declaimed only yesterday. I sat on the wooden bench and looked up at the sky. It was still cloudy, but no rain had fallen. Could fate—or the ancient prophecy—be waiting, weighing Father's actions, holding the skies in readiness? If he was brave, rain would fall and the cure would be found, but if he wasn't, the cure would remain hidden and the skies would clear.

I watched a butterfly flit above the grass that poked up between the cracks in the paving stones. The butterfly flew off, and I stared at the ground. I don't know how long I stared, not thinking, feeling nothing.

Eventually I lifted my head. The afternoon was over. The grapevines and the fountain stood out in the distilled light of dusk. The evening air was chilly, and I shivered.

"Sorcerers' cloaks are very warm."

I jumped.

Rhys draped his cloak over my shoulders. "It's often cold when we fly."

"Thank you."

Had he been watching me for long? I wondered. No. Why would he?

I pulled the cloak close. It felt as warm as wool and as soft as velvet.

He came around to my side of the bench. "I have something to tell you. I've spoken with Orne, my teacher. I told him that Princess Meryl is sick."

His teacher knew the cure! I sprang up. "Did he tell—"

"I didn't mean to raise your hopes." Rhys looked woebegone. "Orne didn't know how to help her, but he said, 'The wind is shifting in Bamarre.' I asked him what that meant, but he only repeated it. I think it must be something good, because he almost smiled as he said it, and he almost never almost smiles."

The wind . . . Maybe the shifting wind would bring the rain! And maybe something could be done to help the wind.

"Rhys? Remember yesterday when you made the cloud music and you made rain fall from a cloud? Could you make rain fall everywhere?"

"No. I wish I could. It's a wonderful idea."

"Could Orne?"

He shook his head.

"Could all the sorcerers together?"

"If there were clouds everywhere, which there wouldn't be, and if there were enough sorcerers, which there aren't. I can draw rain from only a few clouds at a time. Orne can command a mile of clouds, which is amazing." Rhys looked amazed, but then his shoulders slumped. "But it wouldn't be enough. I'm sorry, Princess Addie."

"Never mind." I sat down again.

"Princess Meryl is extraordinary," he said. "If anyone can overcome the Gray Death, she can."

"That's what I think," I said, although I no longer knew what I thought. "I wonder if Trina overcame it."

He didn't say anything. I turned to him, and his face gave him away.

"She died, didn't she?"

He nodded.

"Oh." Poor Trina. I wondered if she had tried my method at all.

"Princess Addie . . ." Rhys spoke rapidly, pacing back and forth across the courtyard. "I just thought of something. The cure prophecy could be fulfilled even if the king fails. It could be fulfilled, and you might not even know it."

"How?"

"A stranger fifty miles from here could find courage. . . ."

There are hundreds of cowards in Bamarre, I thought. Thousands. "That's true."

"What's more, the rain could fall late at night. It needn't rain for more than a minute." He smiled triumphantly.

I smiled back, feeling a bit more cheerful.

His smiled widened. But smiling mustn't have been enough. He rose three feet in the air.

Then his face changed, and he came down. "It's late. I must find your father's camp. He'll be expecting me." He bowed, then launched himself. In a moment he vanished into the darkening sky.

The wind is shifting in Bamarre.

The prophecy had to come true sometime. Why not now?

The wind blew cold, and I pulled the cloak tighter. Rhys's cloak! I still had it. I hugged it to me and left the garden.

The next day was cloudy yet again. Meryl paced ten laps in her bedchamber and then had to lie down. She tried to go to the dining hall at noon but was unable to walk as far as the grand staircase. She failed again to lift Blood-biter using only one arm, but she could still lift it with two.

It was unbearable to watch these minute accomplishments, to smile encouragement, when I wanted to hold her and squeeze her so tightly that my strength would flow into her.

My only consolation was that she was in no pain. She joked grimly that the Gray Death just killed, it never hurt.

Rhys returned early in the afternoon. He reported that Father had quartered the distance to Queen Seema's castle. He and his retinue had thus far been untroubled by monsters. Father had forgotten his slippers, and Rhys was to bring them that evening.

On Sunday we saw the sun, although a few fluffy clouds remained. I told myself that sunshine didn't matter so long as there were still clouds.

In the morning Milton asked Meryl and Bella and me if we'd like to hear an elf tale about Drualt.

"Yes, please!" Meryl said, sitting up a bit straighter.

Milton put his knitting down and went to the middle of the room. "We begin all our stories with these words: 'Good health to you,' and the same words are the refrain. Here is the tale." He folded his hands over his little belly and began.

"Good health to you.

"It was spring and time for Queen Iola to bless the moily herb. She repaired to the field with her handmaidens.

"The sky turned black.

"Queen Iola heard the beating of many wings.

"A hundred gryphons blotted out the sun, cawing and screeching, flapping and wheeling."

Milton flapped his arms and ran a few zigzagging steps, completely failing to look greedy or fierce. Meryl watched, smiling.

I thought, Thank you, Milton, for giving us a moment that has nothing to do with the Gray Death.

He took up the story again. The gryphons descended. Some feasted on the elves' picnic lunch, and some devoured the harvest.

I interrupted. "I thought gryphons ate only flesh."

"No, Addie," Meryl said. "They eat almost anything."

Milton continued,

"Good health to you.

"The gryphons began to feed on Queen

Iola and her attendants.
"A gryphon snapped off the queen's left
thumb as she shielded her youngest
handmaiden."

I clasped my own thumb and held it protec-
tively.

"Good health to you.
"Drualt rode by.
"He galloped to the queen's aid."

The tale went on. Drualt slew several
gryphons and held the rest at bay, while the
queen and her handmaidens retreated to the
queen's castle.

"Good health to you.
"In gratitude, Queen Iola cured Drualt
of a bunion."

Meryl laughed, and I did too. Our hero with
a swollen toe!
The queen asked Drualt how else she
might repay her debt.

"'There is no debt,' Drualt said, 'but
you might nurse King Bruce and his

subjects when they have need.'

"Queen Iola and Drualt never met again, but elves have been nursing humans from that day to this.

"Good health to you."

Milton bowed. We all clapped, even Bella.

"Did the elves really have a queen named Iola?" I asked.

Milton filled a tumbler with water from the pitcher on the washstand and brought it to Meryl.

"Our queen Seema is descended from Queen Iola, and this tale is true. It's written in our *Scroll of Days*."

Meryl and I looked at each other. The elves believed Drualt had lived!

Meryl said, "What do you think, Addie? Do you think it could be true?"

"I don't know," I said. "There could have been a historical Drualt who helped the elves, but the tales in *Drualt* still might be mostly fable."

Bella said, "Drualt never had a bunion, and that's certain."

"Why not?" Meryl said, laughing again. "He had feet, didn't he? If he had a bunion, it would have been the biggest and best one in history. I think the whole story is true, and I think it means that everything in *Drualt* is true too." She beamed at Milton. "Thank you!"

He bowed again and then returned to his knitting.

"Would you like to exercise now?" I asked, hoping that Milton's story might have fortified her.

She was willing, but she paced fewer laps than yesterday, just eight, and she didn't even attempt swordplay. Instead she practiced lifting lighter items—a hairbrush, a hand mirror, and her walking boots. At the end she said she was pleased.

When Rhys came in the afternoon, he said that Father's knights had brought down a gryphon, and there had been jubilation over the killing. He added that the royal party was halfway to Queen Seema.

On Thursday morning, a week after she got sick, Meryl collapsed walking to her wardrobe. Milton had to support her back to bed, with me hovering, aching to help.

She said, "I'll be better soon, Addie. Sir Gray Death hasn't won yet."

I tried to smile, but my expression must have been ghastly.

"Don't look so gloomy. He won the skirmish for my legs, but my heart and my mind have beaten him back a few times already. He won't win out over them."

I tried to believe her, but I didn't. The child specter had only been cruel when it called this an adventure.

Rhys came late that day, almost at dinnertime. Queen Seema had told Father that she knew no cure, nor did she know where a cure might be sought.

"Where will he go now?" Meryl asked. She was in bed, wearing an embroidered robe over her nightdress. I was in the window seat.

Rhys looked down as he answered, "King Lionel is coming home."

Chapter Eleven

"Father is coming home?" I said. "Why?"

Bella said, "He should be here with his child."

My voice rose. "What about *Homely Truths* and rooting out the canker?" What about changing from cowardly to brave?

Rhys answered, still looking at the floor. "He said that *Homely Truths* had told him to seek counsel. He's returning to consult with his councillors." He raised his head and looked at us. "I couldn't argue with him."

He was right, of course. An apprentice sorcerer couldn't harangue a king.

"I never thought he'd find the cure," Meryl said calmly, settling deeper into her pillows. "It doesn't matter."

I was furious with Father for giving up and angry at myself for expecting anything from him.

"One of the knights had a mishap with a specter," Rhys said.

Meryl sat up. "What happened?"

I shivered. Another specter!

Rhys leaned against the mantel. "The king and his retinue were camped outside the walls of Queen Seema's castle, a quarter mile from the ocean cliffs. One of the knights, Sir Osbert, couldn't sleep and went for a walk. He hadn't gone far when he heard a rustling noise, like the swish of a lady's skirt."

"Was that the specter?" Meryl asked.

"It was. But Sir Osbert saw his sister, who had died five years ago of the Gray Death."

I pictured a specter taking Meryl's shape someday. I wanted to run out of the room.

Rhys went on. "He embraced her and never wondered why she was there. Perhaps her scent bewitched him. The specter had aped the dead maiden's perfume."

The specter told Sir Osbert that none of the Gray Death's victims had really died. Instead, they had been whisked to a hidden place close by, where they lived in comfort.

Rhys said, "The specter led Sir Osbert to the edge of a cliff and kept him from seeing the abyss at his feet. Instead, the poor man saw a grassy field and a pavilion lit by a thousand lanterns. In the lantern light he saw two more figures he knew, his cousin and a childhood friend. He ran toward them—and plunged over the edge."

I cried out. I would have run toward Meryl.

Everyone looked at me. I went to Meryl, and she put her arm around me.

"It came out all right," Rhys said. "A sapling broke his fall."

"Was he hurt?" Milton asked.

"Only bruised and shaken. He was lucky."

Bella said, "My cousin Clara saw a specter once. She also said it had a scent. Cloves and honey, I believe."

"I must leave you," Rhys said. "The king instructed me to tell his councillors of his return, but I came here first." He bowed and left.

I ran out into the corridor. "Rhys!"

He turned and waited for me.

"Now she can hardly walk. How long do you think it will be till the slumber comes?"

"Oh, Princess Addie." He reached out to me, then dropped his hand. "Sometimes people who are sick surprise everyone. Sometimes—"

"How long?"

"A few days. At most a week."

He caught my elbow or I would have fallen. A week! Then nine days of sleep and three days of fever. Nineteen days, and she'd be asleep for nine of them. Nineteen days at best, and I'd lose her forever.

Milton stepped into the corridor. "Your sister wants you, Princess Addie."

When I went back in, Meryl told me she was going to sleep.

I must have looked wild with fear, because she added, "I'm only going to nap. It's not the deep sleep. That's not here yet. Am I right, Milton?"

He nodded.

She was still taking care of me. I managed a smile and gave her a kiss. She turned onto her side and closed her eyes.

I left the room. At the end of the corridor I mounted the stairs that led to the north tower, which had always been Meryl's refuge when she wanted to be alone.

The tower door was heavy. I had to push against it with all my weight to get it open. A week ago Meryl had opened it easily. A ladder led to the tower roof. I climbed up.

I crossed the roof and leaned against the battlement. A wind ruffled my hair, a dry wind straight from the western desert. Was this the shifting wind?

I wished Father were like Drualt. If Drualt's daughter had the Gray Death, Drualt would catch a specter and force the cure out of it. He'd sit on a dragon's hoard and refuse to budge till the dragon answered him. If Meryl were his daughter, he'd carry her in his arms till he found the cure. He'd give it to her on the spot, and she'd be the first to recover. If Meryl were his daughter, he wouldn't *let* her die.

My next thought stunned me, although it was obvious. If I had caught the Gray Death instead of Meryl, she would have begun her quest the moment Milton pronounced my doom. She wouldn't be weeping in Bamarre castle and pinning her hopes on a weak king or a foolish theory.

I should have acted as she would have. I should do so now. I had already wasted six days, perhaps a third of the life Meryl had remaining.

But she would have known what to do. She'd thought about this quest and had studied monsters her whole life. I had no idea where to go, and a monster would slay me before I'd gone ten miles. I might as well leap off this battlement. What good would it serve for both of us to die?

Even if I weren't slain, there was scant chance of success, and I'd miss her last days. She wouldn't want that. She'd want me at her side.

I looked down at the farmland spread below

me—the ripening cornfields, the cattle, a herd of pigs. I could see no hint of the troubles that plagued us.

After she died, my grief would be boundless, and my fear too, without her to protect me. And how would I live knowing I'd done nothing to save her?

She was going to die without having the adventures she'd longed for, all because of her promise to me. She'd postponed her dreams just to set me at ease.

How could I fail to help her, at least to try to help her?

I looked out again at beautiful Bamarre. The day was fading, and the western sky was pink. Haze softened the outlines of the Kilkets to the north. A few clouds cast moving shadows over the pastures around the castle and over the deeper green of the pine forest by Lake Orrinic.

A breeze blew in from the Haun Ocean, salty, moist, bracing. I raised my arms in welcome and put out my tongue to taste it. I breathed three deep breaths.

I would try to save Meryl. Most likely I'd die, but nonetheless I would seek her cure.

Chapter Twelve

I turned away from the battlement and left the tower. On my way downstairs I decided to tell Rhys first. Bella wouldn't want me to go, and I didn't know what Meryl would say, but Rhys would help me if he could.

He was in the dining hall, sitting with Father's councillors. I sat in my usual place and gazed at him, hoping to catch his attention. I didn't have long to wait—he looked my way almost instantly. As soon as he did, I stood and left the hall, hoping he'd follow me out.

He did. "Princess Addie? Did you want me?"

I nodded, and opened my mouth to tell him I was going on the quest, but the words didn't come. As soon as I told him, I'd really have to go. I smiled weakly. This was ridiculous.

"Are you feeling well?"

I nodded again. "I . . . I decided . . . I'm going to search for the cure."

Rhys looked startled. He said nothing, but he looked at me intently.

I couldn't read his expression. "Am I doing right? Do you think I should go?" Why was I asking? I was going.

"I only wish I could go with you. When will you leave?"

Oh, how I wished he could come! "At dawn. When do you have to go to the citadel?"

"My summons will come at midnight."

"Do you think I should go?" I repeated. I half hoped he would give me a reason to stay home and be safe.

"I do think you should go, but . . ." He raised a hand, then let it drop. "But I'll worry."

I was glad. I was a complete fool over him, but I was glad he'd worry.

"I may be able to join your quest, for a while at least. There will be breaks in our ceremony. I may be able to get away. Where will you go?"

"I don't know. Where do you think I should go?" I added, "It's probably hopeless anyway."

He was silent for a moment. "Sorcerers believe that an action taken for the right reasons has an unreasonable chance of success. I think your quest will find you, no matter where you search. If I can leave the citadel, I'll search for you. I'll find you."

Would he find me before a monster killed me?

His face brightened. "I have a thing or two for your quest. Just the things!"

Sorcerer's things? They might give me hope—and help.

He said he'd fetch them from his chamber, and we agreed to meet in the library in a few minutes.

I went directly there and pulled two chairs up to the fire, which was burning brightly. Night had fallen outside, but the gas lamps shed a golden light.

Rhys came in carrying a bundle wrapped in cloth. He sat and began to open it. "Will you tell the king's councillors of your quest?"

I hadn't thought about that. I couldn't tell them, though. "No. They wouldn't let me go. They'd make me wait till Father came home."

"You're right." He smiled approvingly. "Now look."

He held up a length of cloth and shook it out. It was a cloak made of dark-blue cloth. He carried it to a table in semidarkness near the window. Then he returned empty-handed to the fire. I looked back at the table. The cloak was gone.

I gasped and ran to the table. When I got close, I saw that the cloak was there, but it was dim, only a glimmer. I picked it up. "What? How?"

I hugged it to me and returned to my seat. The fabric felt substantial. It had weight. But even on my arm, it was hard to see. So was my arm.

"It's not a cloak of invisibility. I wish I had one of those to give you. If you're in bright sunlight, everyone will see you. But if you're in shadow, even in daylight—under a tree, perhaps—and if you stay still, you won't be noticed. At night, no one will see you. The shadow will seem deeper where you are, that's all. It doesn't work on specters and dragons, unfortunately, but ogres and gryphons will be fooled. Humans and sorcerers too."

"Thank you." It might save my life.

Rhys reached into his bundle again. He pulled out more cloth, a large square of linen this time. Every inch was embroidered with images of an elaborate feast.

"A tablecloth." I couldn't imagine what use I'd have for it. "Thank you."

"My pleasure. Now watch. Good tablecloth, please set thyself."

It flew out of his hand and unfolded. It hung in the air, all straight edges and sharp corners, exactly as if a table were beneath it—but I saw no table.

And then! And then!

Dishes began popping out of the empty air and descending on the table with a thump—roast pheasant, roast hare, roast boar, and more—every kind of roast. Every kind of bread too—round loaves and long ones, hard rolls and soft, seeded rolls and plain. Every sort of fish and vegetable and fruit and pastry. Enough food for everyone in the castle, and china plates and silverware to boot.

My eyes must have stood out a foot from my face, because Rhys was laughing.

"Is it real food?" I whispered. "Can one eat it?"

"Try it. Everything is delicious."

I picked up a fork.

Rhys added, "But take care. A man I know stuffed himself so full, he was sick for a week."

The silver fork was heavier than our best cutlery. I loaded it with a big bite of blueberry tart, my favorite treat.

"Mmm. It's lovely." I put down the fork.

"Do you want anything else?"

I shook my head.

Rhys said, "Good tablecloth, I thank thee for a fine meal."

The food and crockery rose above the table. I watched carefully and saw them shrink so fast that they seemed to pop out of sight.

"Everything shrank!" I waved my hand in the air above the tablecloth. It felt like ordinary air. "Is the air filled with roasts and tarts so tiny you can't see them?"

The tablecloth folded itself, and Rhys gave it to me. "I don't think so." He laughed. "But how would anyone tell?"

I laughed too, but I was surprised a sorcerer couldn't tell.

"You have to say the words precisely as I did—'Good tablecloth, please set thyself' and—"

The tablecloth leaped out of my arms.

Rhys added hastily, "And then, 'Good tablecloth, I thank thee for a fine meal.'"

It hung in the air for a moment and then started to fall, but I caught it.

"Remember—if you add a word or leave one out, nothing will happen."

I repeated the words, doubting that the magic would work for me. It did, however. It was a wonderful gift. I would have food on my quest—unless I became food first.

But I knew I mustn't think that way. The tablecloth would keep me fed, and the cloak would keep me safe.

I sat again. "Thank you. Your gifts are marvelous."

"And these . . ." He reached into his bundle again, although it was now quite flat. "Look." He handed me a thin stack of parchment papers.

I took them on my lap and held up the top one to catch the light. "It's a map of the Eskerns!" I peered at it. The markings were thin and spidery, but clear if I looked closely. Ogres' camps dotted the slopes. I caught my breath. So many! And gryphon nests capped the peaks. Not every peak, but many. I would need my magic cloak in the Eskerns.

"The maps aren't magical," Rhys said. "Apprentice sorcerers draw them."

I put the map of the Eskerns aside and picked up another one.

He went on. "Some maps are older than others, and the old ones may not be completely accurate. Monsters move. New monsters are born."

The next map was of Bamarre castle and the land around it. There were the farms, Lake Orrinic and its nearby cave, and the pine forest. I saw a word along the southeastern fringe of the forest: *Specters*. The spectral child had been in the west, however, so they'd spread westward since the map had been drawn.

The next map was of the Kilkets. There were seven maps in all: Mulee Forest; the western desert where the dragons dwell; the ocean shore and the elf queen's castle; the sorcerers' citadel and the plains around it, which were in southwestern Bamarre, between the desert and Mulee Forest.

"Is there a map of Mount Ziriat and how to reach it?" I'd take the quest straight to the fairies if I could.

"We don't know where the mountain is. It's invisible to us too. Occasionally a fairy or two visits the elders, but I'm not privy to why they come or what they say." He was quiet. "I would love to see a fairy."

"I would too."

We smiled at each other. Wistful smiles.

If I died, I'd never see him again.

But I wasn't going to die.

"Never mind about the fairies." I tapped the maps. "These are the best gifts of all."

"I wish they were perfectly reliable. I wish . . ." He shrugged, looking unhappy.

I didn't want to end by weeping. "I'll find the cure and come back fat from your marvelous tablecloth." I stood on tiptoe and kissed him on the cheek. "Thank you." Then I blushed at my audacity.

He looked startled, and then solemn. My last sight of him: He was bowing.

Chapter Thirteen

On the way to my chamber I realized I couldn't tell Bella and Milton about my quest, because they might think it their duty to tell Father's councillors.

But I wanted to tell them. I blinked back tears. I wanted their advice. Bella knew a thousand tales of monsters, and some of her lore might help me, and Milton might have useful elvish counsel. More than that, though, I wanted them to follow me with their eyes as I prepared to leave. I wanted to feel their love, to carry it away with me.

I'd tell Meryl late tonight, when she was alone. She wasn't so sick yet that she needed an elf through the night.

In my room I wrote a letter to Father.

"Sire," I wrote, "your valiant attempt to save my sister has moved me to emulation. I cannot let her die without trying, as you did, to save her. I am leaving on a quest for her salvation and the cure to the Gray Death. I consulted *The*

Book of Homely Truths, and it spoke to me with these words. . . ."

I took my copy down from the shelf in my wardrobe and thumbed through it. "Peril recollected is superior to peril evaded." Not quite right. "The sickroom is a battlefield; take command or forfeit." Not right either. Ah. "An endeavor undertaken in the fullness of need is its own imperative." I didn't know exactly what it meant, but it seemed urgent and portentous enough.

I copied down the moral and continued, "Please do not send a party after me, lest you go against the wisdom of *Homely Truths* and bring trouble down on us both. If I do not return, I hope you will remember me as a dutiful and respectful daughter."

I'd give the note to Meryl to deliver when Father returned. I sat in my window seat and watched the starry sky, and fell asleep. At midnight I awoke. I stood and stretched.

Meryl was lying on her side, facing me as I opened her door. Moonlight poured in her window, and I saw that her eyes were open. She smiled at me. "I was thinking about you. I was thinking—"

"I came to tell you. I'm leaving Bamarre castle."

"Where are you going?" She struggled to sit up.

I hurried to her.

"Don't help me." She panted. "There." She straightened her shoulders and sat erect. "That's better. Where are you going?"

Tears streamed down my face. What if I never saw her again? "I'm going to find the cure."

"You'd leave home for me?" I heard tears in her voice. "Oh, Addie."

We hugged and didn't speak for a few minutes.

Finally she whispered bitterly, "Sir Gray Death robbed me of my adventure and gave it to you."

I hugged her harder. "He has a lot to answer for."

She said, sounding more like herself, "We'll make him regret it." She pulled out of my arms and looked at me. "You'll have a better chance than Father. You'll put your whole self into it, and that will help you." She thought for a minute, and then her face lit up. "You can take Blood-biter. It will help you too." She shrugged. "At least I threatened your specter with it. I used it that much."

I took the sword down from the mantelpiece

and put it on the floor by the door. How would I use it? I knew nothing about swordplay.

"Where would you have gone on your quest for the cure?"

She smiled. "Everywhere, since it was to be a grand adventure. But first I would have looked for fairies."

"How?"

"I was planning to catch a specter and ask it how to find them. When are you leaving? Tomorrow morning?"

I nodded and gave her my note to Father.

"What did Bella say?"

"I haven't told Bella, and you mustn't either."

"You have to tell her. She'll never forgive you if you don't. She won't tell anyone she shouldn't. Besides, you can order her not to. She'll help you. Tell Milton too."

I didn't argue. We said good-bye and hugged again. I might have continued to hold her for the next nineteen days, but she said, "Go, Addie. I need sleep to do battle again tomorrow."

I started for the door.

She said, "You're the bravest sister in Bamarre."

"I wish I were brave." I went back and hugged her one more time. "I wish I were like you." I picked up Blood-biter and ran out.

I stopped at the bottom of the staircase that led to Bella's bedchamber. It was time for me to think for myself, and I thought it best and safest not to tell Bella or Milton.

But I had the guilty feeling that Meryl was hearing my thoughts.

In my room I fell asleep instantly and slept deeply.

I awoke before dawn. My first adventure was going to be slipping out of the castle and crossing the drawbridge unnoticed. I picked out my plainest gown. It was finer than I liked, but it would have to do.

I packed my things into my sewing basket. I put fresh underclothes on the bottom, and above them the maps, the magic cloak, and the magic tablecloth. On top I placed my worn copy of *Drualt*. I selected two gold brooches, which I could trade for money if I needed to. They were small, and I feared they might fall out of the basket, so I pinned them to my shift. Last of all I buried Rhys's first gift, the wooden ball holding the beautiful cloth, at the bottom of the basket. I didn't need it, but I couldn't leave it behind.

As I packed, I didn't think about my quest. I didn't think about my fears. I didn't even think about where I would go first. I only worked, in time with my pounding heart.

My eyes fell on Blood-biter. How would I—

Someone tapped on my door. I thrust the basket into the bottom of my wardrobe. Then I hurried to the door and opened it a crack. Milton was there.

"Meryl! She's worse!" I opened the door to admit him.

He shook his head and came in. "No worse. I didn't mean to frighten you." He lifted himself onto the chair next to my wardrobe.

"I woke early and looked in on Princess Meryl. She told me you're leaving to—"

"Did you tell anyone?"

"Just Bella."

"Is she going to the councillors?"

"No. She only said that she had something for you, and so do I. Here, my dear." He held a leather pouch out to me.

The scent reached me before I opened it— clean as mint, sweet and rich as lilacs. Inside were tiny dried purple flowers. I turned to Milton, puzzled.

He smiled. "It's our moily herb. Our moily herb will give you heart. Put a flower in your tea and you'll find the strength to go on. If you have no tea, pop one in your mouth and suck on it."

"Thank you. I'll—"

Bella rushed in, still wearing her nightdress and cap. A gown was draped over one arm, and she carried a lumpy-looking canvas sack. She stopped abruptly and stood uncertainly, looking up at the ceiling, down at the floor—anywhere but at me. Then she started to cry.

"I have to go," I said. "I have to."

She nodded. "Here, put this on." She handed me the gown.

It was made of rough muslin in a bright green that I never would have chosen. With its canary-yellow apron it befit a jaunty serving maid, one who was shorter and stouter than I. But it would help me leave the castle undetected.

"And you can carry your things in this." She lifted the sack.

It would be better than my basket, which had no cover.

"These may be of use too. Best be careful, though." She reached into the sack and pulled out a pair of worn black boots.

"My, they're big," Milton said.

They were big enough for one of the royal guards, and I was already wearing my riding boots, which were very sturdy.

"They're more than they seem. They're

seven-league boots." She reached into the sack again. "This goes with them."

I didn't understand. "What are seven-league boots?" Why did a spyglass go with them?

"Your mother left them for you and Meryl." Bella wiped her eyes and sniffled. "She said that the boots go seven leagues when you take a step. I don't know what the spyglass is for."

"Why didn't you give them to us before?"

Bella's face turned red. "They weren't proper for princesses, and Meryl would have used them." Her face crumpled. "Now it doesn't matter."

Meryl would have loved them. Bella and I both had kept Meryl from her deepest wishes.

"Thank you." I pushed the boots and the spyglass back into the sack and added my things from the basket.

Meryl had been right to tell Milton. She'd been my protective sister one more time.

I used one of the brooches to pin the pouch of moily herbs to my shift. Then I looked at Blood-biter, leaning against my washstand.

I was no warrior, but it was Meryl's gift. I put it into the sack too. It just fit. I was barely able to close the sack's drawstring. I hoped the scabbard wouldn't poke through the cloth.

"Where will you go?" Bella asked.

I shrugged. Rhys had said the quest would find me. I hoped he was right, because I couldn't see beyond crossing the drawbridge. I could hardly see that far.

Chapter Fourteen

Milton said he'd fly a gray pennant from the highest tower if Meryl entered another phase of the Gray Death. He told me to use the spyglass to see it. I hugged him good-bye.

Bella hugged me. "Dragons and specters *know* things." She hiccoughed from crying too long. "But find someone else to question them. Not you."

I didn't go into Meryl's room again. I knew that if I did, I'd never leave.

I crossed the drawbridge on foot. No one recognized me. A man bumped into me and didn't apologize. A woman called me a lazy lump because I wasn't walking fast enough to suit her.

On the far side of the bridge I turned off the road onto one of the farmers' tracks where Meryl, Bella, and I often rode. A hot breeze rattled through the wheat fields around me. Above, a flock of red geese wheeled and beat the air, honking steadily.

When I was out of sight of the road, I

stopped and put down my sack, which had grown heavy. I sat in the dusty track to consider where to go. Meryl's favorite lines from *Drualt* came to me.

> *Step follows step.*
> *Hope follows courage.*
> *Set your face toward danger.*
> *Set your heart on victory.*

I was terrified of specters, but I was even more afraid of dragons, so I decided to go to Mulee Forest first. No humans lived there, so anyone I met would be a specter. To be certain, I'd enter the forest at night, wearing my magic cloak, which would conceal me from all but specters—and dragons, if any were near.

I'd never reach the Mulee in time without Mother's gift, the seven-league boots. I took the spyglass out of my sack. I had realized why it went with the boots—so I could see where I was going, so I wouldn't step into the middle of an ocean or a mountain.

I wondered if Meryl had awakened yet. This would be my first day ever without her.

I examined the spyglass. Behind the eyepiece were three rings. The first had notches numbered from one to fifty. In tiny flowing script the legend read *Seven Leagues*. I assumed that each notch increased the distance viewed by seven leagues. Thus I calculated that the greatest distance the spyglass could show me was three hundred fifty leagues, or a thousand fifty miles. Far enough and more.

The next ring was labeled *Miles*, and it was numbered from one to twenty-one. The third ring was neither marked nor labeled.

Mulee Forest was about three hundred miles away. I set the leagues ring at sixteen, faced south, and put the eyepiece to my eye.

The forest was dark as dusk. The trees were huge, so close together that I had no vista. Thick vines hung between them and trailed on the forest floor. The spyglass didn't show the vines clearly—they were blurred. On the ground were bright butter-yellow flowers, blurry too, but still dots of sunshine in the forest's twilight.

It was a restful scene, nothing frightening. A burst of purple, unclear as well, flashed by and settled on a low branch. I knew it was a bird, but I wished I could see it better.

I put my fingers around the unmarked ring and twisted. The scene became clear.

Oh no! A hairy brown spider clung to a vine!

I couldn't go there!

I'd go to the desert to find a dragon. I began to reset the spyglass, but then I stopped myself. A spider was worse than a dragon?

No.

My first monsters would be spiders, then. My fingers trembled, but I unlaced my ordinary boots and took the magic ones out of my sack.

The sole of the right boot was flapping, and the left heel was half worn away. Even worse, the boots were so big, I feared they'd fall off during my first step.

I slipped my foot into a boot—and it shrank to a perfect fit. Thank you for your gift, Mother.

I set the spyglass's seven-league ring to the first notch and looked to see where my step would take me. A lake. I didn't want to begin by drowning. I turned my head slightly and looked again. A village. I turned more. A pasture with sheep. Perfect. I clutched my sack and stood, placing my feet carefully and not moving them.

My quest was beginning.

I raised the spyglass and lifted my right foot. Meryl, I will save you.

A horse in harness turned into the track a few feet ahead of me. The horse reared in surprise. I stumbled back. The boots whizzed away and me with them, going in the wrong direction. I glimpsed the farmer's startled face and then I was gone, hurtling backward.

I was a rag doll dragged by a whirlwind, my feet inches above the ground, bouncing into rocks, dirt—too fast to see. Crossed a stream, a marsh—over a fence—inches from a stone fort—whipping wind, dust, leaves, thorns, bushes, mud.

The boots slowed down jerkily and stopped on a hill. But I couldn't catch my balance. I went on stumbling and was off again.

I fought for control so I'd be able to stay where I was when this step was over. While I skimmed over the rough ground—more rocks, tall grass, a road, a river—I struggled to raise my arms. My left hand still held the spyglass, and my right clutched my sack.

After about three minutes the boots slowed. I crashed into something and fell to my knees. For a moment I was pleased that I had truly stopped. Then I saw what I had struck against.

An ogre. Huge—twice my height and five times broader. For a moment I stared stupidly at him and he stared stupidly at me. Then I began to scramble away, on my knees. I should have stood and used the boots, but my mind was a blur of fear.

He grinned and grabbed my left arm. I tried to pull free, but I couldn't. He said something.

His voice was like rocks colliding. Other colliding rocks answered him. He had three companions, all grinning, their lipless mouths making long cracks in their pasty faces.

The ogre holding me picked up his club and raised it. My wits returned. I stood and took a step.

The ogre came with me! I was dragging him! My arm was going to be ripped away. My shoulder was a blaze of pain.

It was worse to see the world rush at me. A stone wall! I braced myself and bumped over it. A stand of trees! We crashed between them, cracking branches and scattering leaves.

I glanced back. The ogre was trying to shield himself with his free arm. His face was purple, his eyes wild.

The boots slowed and then stopped. The ogre roared and raised his club. I took another step, shrieking from the agony in my shoulder.

How long could I pull him?

Far ahead to my left—a lookout tower. We'd pass it by, unless . . . I leaned to my left as hard as I could. The boots changed direction, just a bit. I kept leaning. The ogre's roar changed pitch, whined, squealed. The tower was seconds away. Aaah! I was going to hit it!

Chapter Fifteen

I found a shred of strength and forced myself more to the right. The ogre slammed into the tower, and I broke free and sped on. About a minute later, the boots slowed, and I threw myself to the ground. The pain in my shoulder filled the world.

The sleeve of my gown had torn away from the bodice, so I could see my skin, which was livid—black and purple and orange. My shoulder and arm were swelling. My sleeve was already too tight, adding another note to my pain. I could move my fingers, but I couldn't raise my arm. I was sure the bone in my arm had been pulled out of my shoulder socket. I wished for Milton.

I closed my eyes. I could do nothing while this pain lasted.

Milton! Maybe his gift, the moily herb, would help me. I unpinned the pouch from my shift and succeeded in opening it with my good hand. The scent of the herb was soothing. I put a flower on my tongue. Its aroma filled my mouth, and for a sweet moment I was free of pain. Then the pain returned, but it no longer overwhelmed me.

I lay back and fell into a swoon. I dreamed of a friend who came to me from the north. I knew he was a friend, although I'd never seen him before. Yet I was terribly glad to see him *again*.

He sat by me and eased off the sleeve of my gown. Then he gently guided the bone in my arm back into the embrace of my shoulder.

For a moment I thought he might be Rhys, but then I knew he wasn't.

The dream faded and I opened my eyes. The afternoon was half over, and the pain in my shoulder had shrunk to a dull ache. My arm was bare, still swollen, but less than before. I even felt well enough to be hungry.

The sleeve of my gown lay crumpled a few feet away from me. The boots leaned against my sack, although I had no recollection of taking them off. They had expanded and again appeared much too big for my feet.

They were dangerous transportation. But they had enabled me to get rid of the ogre. I sat up. I had killed an ogre, or at the least I had wounded him terribly, and he would be a long while healing. I grinned. I, Addie the fearful, Addie the shy, had prevailed against an *ogre*!

I knew how Drualt felt when he vanquished a foe. I had never known before, but now I knew why Drualt was called the laugher.

> *Drualt, the laugher,*
> *Laughed at the sun*
> *On his shield,*
> *The moon in his silver sword,*
> *The drum in his heart.*
> *Laughed at his someday death*
> *Glimpsed from afar.*
> *Drualt, the laugher,*
> *Laughed at laughing.*

Addie, the laugher.

I wished I could tell Meryl.

Meryl—I was suddenly certain that something terrible had happened—that the sleep had come, or something worse. I raised the spyglass.

No gray pennant flew. I let out the breath I'd been holding.

I wondered if the spyglass could penetrate the castle walls and I could see her. I lowered it ever so slightly and found myself staring at the northwestern castle wall. But Meryl's chamber and my own faced east. I twisted the third metal ring, and now I was peeping into a servant's small chamber. The spyglass could see through stone and wood! I twisted again and found a corridor. It took a few minutes, but I found Meryl. She was in her nightdress, seated in her blue chair, a tray of food in her lap. She looked no worse.

Bella leaned forward in the red chair, probably urging her to eat. I wished for a magical glass for my ears, and another that I could speak into. A listenglass and a speakglass.

I lowered the spyglass. Locating our castle had told me how far I had gone and where I was. I had taken two boot steps north and two more to the west. I was on the Bamarrian Plains, and the river at my feet was the same Byne that fed our moat at home.

The river was narrower here, and lazier. On the opposite shore five cows grazed. Downstream a willow trailed its branches in the water. I took Rhys's maps out of my sack. There were villages along the Byne. I could find one and spend the night at an inn. There would be no ogres at an inn.

And waste the rest of the day? I couldn't. Besides—I looked down at myself—I wouldn't be admitted at a respectable inn. My skirts were stained and muddy. The hem was shredded, and there was a tear all the way up to my knee.

An inn was impossible, but before I risked myself in Mulee Forest, I had to eat. I dug in my sack again and pulled out the magic tablecloth.

It felt silly to address a tablecloth. "Good tablecloth, please set thyself."

It shook itself out, and a meal appeared, precisely enough for me, not the absurd abundance the tablecloth had displayed before. There were cool sweet pea soup, roasted sea bream, and for dessert mulberry pudding. Foods I loved.

I picked up the soupspoon, and the cloth that hung down the side of the nonexistent table *shoved* me! I stumbled back and found myself seated. There was no chair that I could see, but I felt as if I were sitting on a thin cushion over a wooden seat. I reached down. The cushion had an invisible fringe, and beneath the cushion I touched wood, or so it seemed. I thought I felt the grain, and it occurred to me to be careful of splinters, since an invisible splinter might prove impossible to remove.

Hunger took over. I forgot about the chair and ate. I finished every bite and said with utter sincerity, "Good tablecloth, I thank thee for a fine meal."

It folded itself and hung in the air for a moment before starting to fall. I caught it and returned it to my sack.

The sun was low in the sky. I put the boots on again, grabbed up my sack, and aimed the spyglass south at the forest. If I had overcome an ogre, I could overcome a specter. I took a step.

It was less frightening now that I knew I could control my direction. I found that I had the greatest effect when the boots began to slow.

On the fourth step I would have landed in a lake if I hadn't steered. But I avoided disaster and began to enjoy myself. It was exhilarating to whoosh along, to see the plains grow into hills and shrink again to plains. For a moment the boots swept me along a road. I rushed toward a line of wagons. As I passed them, I saw the terrified face of the lead driver.

In the middle of the sixteenth step I entered Mulee Forest. Oh no! I could never avoid all these trees. I was going to be dashed to death.

However, the boots knew their business. I was knocked about, and my gasping mouth filled with leaves, but I wasn't much hurt. The boots slowed at last, and I threw myself on the ground. I spit out the leaves and sat up, looking for spiders.

I saw none and began to breathe again.

I removed the seven-league boots and replaced them with my ordinary ones. The forest was quiet, probably shocked into silence by my arrival. If specters had ears, and I didn't know if they did, every one of them would know I was here. Well, I had come to find a specter. I wanted them to know.

The trees around me were Bamarrian locusts from which hung the hairy vines I had seen in the spyglass. The ground was soft, layered with decades, probably centuries, of dead leaves. Between the locusts grew tall stalks topped with waxy red flowers, unnaturally bright in this shadow land.

The noise of the forest resumed. A lark sang, sounding as sweet and lovely as any lark at home. Insects whirred and droned. A woodpecker drummed. I heard rustling in the underbrush. I stayed still and waited, my pulse racing, but nothing came at me.

The air was damp and chilly. I found the cloak in my sack, wrapped myself in it, and was warmed in an instant.

I didn't know what to do next. I was here, and I had thought that would be enough.

"Here I am," I finally called. "Come find me." My voice sounded high-pitched and brittle. It hung in the air, and I waited for it to crack and clatter to the ground.

I imagined specters behind every tree, laughing at me—at my hopes, my intentions, my folly in entering their domain. They'd be pleased if Meryl died. They'd be delighted to cause my death too.

I began to walk, watching for specters and spiders. "Here I am. Come to me."

Nothing came. I walked on, although I was exhausted and my shoulder had begun to throb.

Luck was with me. I saw no spiders.

Luck was against me. I saw no specters.

The forest scene hardly changed. I passed from locusts to oaks to hemlocks, and the flowers were different, but the vines remained the same, and the murky light never diminished, even though night must have fallen outside the forest.

Just when I was too tired to take another step, I came to a glade. I collapsed on a carpet of moss and looked up. High above me there was a break in the ceiling of leaves. I saw a dark sky and three stars.

That sky and those stars were a great comfort. They were the world outside the forest. I smiled up at them. I had tried hard today. I could do no more without rest.

I tucked my sack under my head for a pillow, stretched out, and was asleep in an instant.

Chapter Sixteen

"Princess Addie?"

It was Rhys's voice. I struggled out of a deep sleep. Rhys! I woke up completely. "Is Meryl worse?" I sat up, drawing the cloak tighter around me for warmth.

"She's the same."

The sky was still dark, but I saw him clearly in the ghostly light of the forest.

He crouched over me. "I didn't mean to frighten you."

I smiled at his anxious expression. I was so glad to see him.

"You hurt your arm!"

"It's nothing. I only rid myself of an ogre," I said, unable to resist boasting.

He bowed by way of congratulation. "I have news myself," he said. "About the cure."

I jumped up. "You found it?"

"Not *the* cure, but *a* cure. It's here in the forest. Under the forest, anyway. I'll tell you about it on our way there."

I picked up my sack. "I'm ready."

He took the sack from me, and we set out. The forest was quieter than before. I heard rustling and the occasional crack of a twig breaking, but no birdsong. I wondered what time it was.

Often there wasn't room enough to walk side by side, so Rhys followed me, guiding me with his hand on my elbow. His touch was a comfort—more than a comfort.

I even stopped worrying about spiders. If I saw one, Rhys would know what to do.

As we went, he explained how he'd come upon the special cure. His first day at the citadel had ended at midday, and he was free until tomorrow afternoon. He'd gone to Bamarre castle to see how Meryl fared. Then he'd set out to find me, and on his way he'd met a dwarf.

"I walked a way with him," he said. "I'd never met a tipsy dwarf before, Addie . . . Princess Addie. This fellow had quaffed too much ale, and it loosened his tongue."

The dwarf had told Rhys about the dwarfs' great ceremony, which was held once in every two centuries. Rhys explained that most dwarfs live two hundred years. Their queen, however, lives forever, one lifetime after another. Each time she becomes old and begins to die, the dwarfs carry her on a jeweled palanquin through hundreds of miles of underground passages to a place deep below Mulee Forest.

Rhys's voice was hushed. I looked back and saw that he was wide-eyed, filled with the drama of the great event. "They sing as they go to keep the queen's spirits up. Isn't that grand?"

"Yes," I whispered.

"Finally they reach a secret chamber, their most sacred place. The walls are encrusted with precious stones, and there is a golden altar. Atop the altar is a small oaken box, and in the box is a plain silver ring. A dwarf prince places the ring on the dying queen's finger, and she begins to revive. After she has worn it for an hour, she removes it. She needs it no longer because she has been restored to good health for another two hundred years. Then the celebration begins."

"But it's a charm for dwarfs, not humans," I said tentatively, not understanding. "And the queen never has the Gray Death."

"I thought so too, Addie . . . Princess Addie." He stopped walking, and I stopped as well, or he would have lost his hold on my arm. "In my thoughts you are always Addie, simply Addie."

In his thoughts! He thought of me when I wasn't there?

I stammered, "You may c-call me Addie, simply Addie."

"Addie . . . Ah, that comes more easily." He pushed gently on my arm, and we began to walk again. "As I was saying, *Addie*, the dwarf told me that the ring cured royalty, any royalty, and of any disease."

I thought about it. "But shouldn't we go to the queen and ask to borrow the ring? It wouldn't take long to get there with my boots, and you could fly."

Rhys let go of my arm. I turned.

He was standing still, looking distressed. "That would be right, and that's how we should do it, only it takes weeks to get an audience with the queen. But if we go directly to the secret chamber, we can borrow the ring and return it, all in a few hours."

I considered it. The ring could save Meryl, perhaps today. I pictured her well again, thanking Rhys and me, whirling Bella around the room, brandishing Blood-biter. "As soon as Meryl is cured, the three of us could return the ring and then thank the dwarf queen."

Rhys nodded enthusiastically. "We'll do it—"

Someone in the distance called my name. "Did you hear that?" I asked.

"No." He paused, listening. "Hear what?"

"Someone called me. It came from that direction." I pointed to my right. It had been a man's voice, but I didn't recognize it.

"Is that the first time you've heard it?"

"Yes. The first time."

"The Mulee is full of phantom sounds, noises to lure you into danger. You may hear it again."

"Is it a specter?"

"It must be, but this deep in the forest you won't catch it. If you follow the voice, it will only lead you to your death."

Let us find the ring quickly and leave this place, I thought. I began walking again. "How do we get down to the secret chamber?"

"There is an entryway. The dwarf described it, and I found it. It's not far. I would have retrieved the ring myself, but the dwarf said the charm would be broken if anyone approached the chamber who was neither dwarf nor royal. I'll guard the entrance. I saw several murky shapes lurking about when I was there."

We walked on in silence for a few minutes. I thought about the dwarf queen. I said, "I'm—"

At the same moment, he said, "Addie—"

We stopped speaking, confused. Rhys said

gallantly, "Tell me, and I shall wait." His hand twitched on my arm, and I thought he was battling the impulse to bow.

I smiled. "I was about to say that I'm surprised the queen never came forward with the ring when my mother was sick, but perhaps she didn't think of it."

"It's the only explanation. She wouldn't mean any harm."

"What were you going to say?"

"Hmm. I was going to say that I learned something from Orne today. He—"

"About the Gray Death?"

"No. It's about Orne himself. Perhaps I shouldn't mention it now."

"Please tell me."

"It's this." He cleared his throat. "No sorcerer is sterner than Orne. None is less interested in the world beyond his sorcery, yet yesterday Orne confessed to me that he once was wed to a human! Three hundred years ago, he said."

Rhys's teacher, the one likeliest to influence him, wed to a human!

I heard the phantom voice again, calling my name. And again. "Princess Addie, Princess Addie." It sounded so real.

"I thought he didn't care for humans, but he told me how sweet his wife was."

I stumbled over a tree root. Rhys tightened his grip on my arm and saved me from falling.

"Then Orne added something astonishing. He said that all the best sorcerers had once been devoted to another creature, a human, elf, or dwarf." Rhys paused. "But then he wouldn't say another word on the subject. He only warned me not to neglect my studies."

Too much was happening at once. And there was that voice again, calling me, reminding me how fearful a place Mulee Forest was.

"I meant not to say a word of this," Rhys said. "I'm not much of a sorcerer if I can't command my own lips."

I wished he'd told me later, after Meryl . . . after Meryl was cured—only a few hours from now, if I found the ring!

With Meryl cured, I'd be delighted about Orne's wife—and I'd be able to wonder what it meant for me.

"Are we near the entrance?" I said.

"Quite near. Addie?" He paused. "May I speak of this—Orne's marriage and, um, related matters . . . may I speak again at a better time?"

The answer was yes. It could be nothing

else, but I wished he'd stop for now. "I don't know. I suppose."

He fell silent at last. I wondered how long we'd been walking. I couldn't measure time in this unchanging half-light.

"Ah. Here we are."

I saw no entrance, just a pile of rocks, boulders almost. Rhys took out his baton and pointed it at the topmost, biggest rock, which lifted and floated to the foot of a towering maple tree.

Where the rock had been was now a hole, with steps leading downward. I meant to approach it boldly. But my knees felt weak, so I edged toward it. The opening was wide at the mouth but narrowed quickly. Cold, putrid air streamed from it.

I drew back. "How far is the chamber?"

"The dwarf said the walk was no more than half an hour."

Half an hour, and half an hour to return. An hour in that tunnel! "How will I see my way?"

"I can give you light, but I don't like your going in there alone. Perhaps we should go to the queen after all."

"We can't. Meryl can't wait."

Rhys tapped his baton twice and held it out

to me. "When you enter the darkness, it will begin to glow."

I took the baton. "If anything happens to me, will you go straight to the queen and beg for an immediate audience?"

He nodded and went on nodding as I added, "If she won't grant it, tell Father. Perhaps she'll see him more quickly."

I crouched over the entrance. A gust of foul air eddied out. I drew the cloak tighter around me and turned back to Rhys. "Couldn't . . ." I was about to ask if he'd come in a short way with me, but I couldn't risk Meryl's life. "I suppose . . . I'll go now."

Rhys looked so worried that it eased my fear a bit.

"Farewell." I lowered my foot to the first step. Icy cold traveled up my leg to my heart. I withdrew my leg. I couldn't go in there.

I had to.

I tried to make myself move, but I stood frozen.

It was absurd. Entering the tunnel was the least dangerous thing I'd done all day. No monsters would be within, and Rhys would guard the entrance.

I took a deep breath—and still failed to

move. I was yet the coward, unable to do what was needed. I turned to Rhys.

"If you think it unsafe," he said, "you mustn't go in there. You can simply go on with your quest."

How would I continue the quest if I couldn't even do this? I put my foot on the first step again, and this time I didn't withdraw it, but I couldn't make my other foot follow. I stood that way for a full five minutes, staring into the darkness, while the hole belched its dank vapors at me.

If I fetched the ring, Meryl would be well and I'd be safe. I'd never have to leave Bamarre castle again if I didn't want to.

My left foot followed my right. I began the descent.

"Princess Addie?"

I turned.

There was another Rhys, sailing between the trees a few yards from me. "Princess Addie? Are you here?" it called. It didn't seem to see me.

A specter! I was about to catch a specter!

"Begone, Monster!" Rhys commanded. "You shall not—"

"No! Wait!" I stepped out of the hole. "Don't leave, you monster," I shouted. "I have a question to ask you." Perhaps I wouldn't have to go in the hole after all.

It turned at the sound of my voice. "Princess Addie? Is that you? I can't see you. Are you wearing your magic cloak?"

Chapter Seventeen

M y cloak! I whipped it off. Only specters and dragons could see me while I wore it. I'd been wandering with a specter! I'd been gulled again.

The spectral Rhys, the monster, the one that had lured me here, began to laugh, sounding high-pitched and cruel. It hugged itself and rocked with laughter. It began to vanish.

"Stay," I said, my voice weak from fright and shock.

It continued to disappear. In a moment it would be gone.

"Stay!" I shouted. "I command you."

It reappeared.

"Tell me how to find the cure to the Gray Death."

The real Rhys took my sack from the specter.

It spoke. "I know nothing of a cure, but dragons and fairies know." It laughed again. "But you'll have an easier time finding a dragon than a fairy." It bowed in a mockery of Rhys's extravagant gesture. Then it vanished. Its baton, which I still held, vanished too, and my fingers closed over air.

I backed away from the hole. For a moment I couldn't speak. Finally I said, "Is Meryl all right? Is she worse?"

"She's unchanged. No weaker."

No weaker. The specter had spoken true, about this at least.

"Are you hurt? Your arm looks—"

"I'm fine." The specter's trap—the tunnel— still menaced. "Can you cover that hole?"

Rhys replaced the rock over the entrance with difficulty, panting from the effort. "This is the worst spot in the forest, I think." He paused to catch his breath. "I found a clearing not far from here. Do you want to go there?"

I nodded and followed him, struggling to overcome my fright.

He turned his head and said, "Orne believes specters are beautiful, but I . . ."

I should have recognized the monster for what it was. Rhys, the real Rhys, would never steal a ring or take advantage of a dwarf's drunkenness.

How did I know *this* Rhys was real? He had saved me from the hole, but he still could be . . . Maybe I was the victim of a scheme among several specters. He too was taking me to a place I didn't know.

I studied his back as I followed him, but it told me nothing.

"The clearing should be very close. Let me see. Ah, yes. Here it is."

Nothing seemed wrong. Again, I was comforted by the sight of the sky. It was still night, but the stars were beginning to fade.

Rhys twirled around to face me, his cloak billowing out behind him. "I'm so glad I found you."

"How did you know where to look?"

"Princess Meryl said she'd told you that specters might know where to find the cure."

That was true. She had said that. For a moment I relaxed, but then I began to doubt again. A specter could know what Meryl had said.

I knelt down and began to clear away dead leaves, working furiously. When she'd caught the specter at Lake Orrinic, Meryl had shown me how to detect the creatures.

"What are you doing, Princess Addie? May I help?"

I ignored him. In a few minutes I had cleared a space. The soil was moist, spongy. I leaned on it with my hand and made a handprint.

I sat back and said, "Stand here."

He looked puzzled but stood where I told him.

"Now step away."

He did—and left no footprints.

"You're . . ." My voice cracked. "You're a specter too. You should have known better than to try to trick me twice."

The monster stood there stupidly. It still had my sack. I reached up and snatched it, and the creature offered no resistance. Clutching the sack tight, I began to pull off my ordinary boots. "So tell me what you know, creature," I panted. Then I shouted, roared, "How fares my sister truly?"

"Princess Addie, I'm no specter." It fell to its knees, clasping its hands dramatically. It played the real Rhys to a fare-thee-well. "What test did I fail?"

I yanked the magic boots out of the sack and pushed my ordinary ones in. "You know the test, and so do I. Now you must answer my question. Tell me true, how fares my sister?" I stuck my right foot into a magic boot—the left magic boot. I pulled the boot off. "Answer me, I command you."

"If I don't answer you, doesn't that prove I'm no specter?"

I sat still. I didn't know. Then I shook my

head. "You proved what you are when you couldn't leave a footprint."

It chuckled. Chuckled! It was having a fine time, toying with me.

"That's the trouble?" it said. "I can leave a footprint, nothing easier." It stepped back into the space I'd cleared, then stepped away, leaving two undeniable boot prints.

"They're the boots, not you. You're a sorcerer. You can do anything. I mean, you're a specter, and you can do anything."

It sat on the ground and began to unlace its boots. "Sorcerers' feet are very ugly, very bony. I would have spared you the sight." It pulled off its hose, which had a big darn at the right heel.

Its toes *were* bony, with a tuft of hair at the knuckles. Its toenails needed trimming. It returned to the cleared spot . . .

And made two glorious footprints.

He was Rhys!

I smiled up at him, flooded with relief. "But why didn't you leave a footprint at first?"

He blushed. "Few humans know this about us." He sat on the ground next to me. "Our natural state is flying or floating in the air, not walking. We're supposed to truly walk and put our weight down when we're with humans. But . . ." His blush deepened. ". . . I cheat. I float a hair's width above the ground." He chuckled. "Don't tell Orne."

Orne! I wondered if the specter had been truthful about him. "Rhys . . . Do you know . . . Did Orne . . . Was your teacher ever married?"

Rhys looked at me quizzically. "Did the specter tell you he had been?"

I blushed. "To a human."

"Orne?" He shook his head. "I doubt it. He's against sorcerers marrying."

I returned the magic boots to my sack and put my ordinary ones on again. I was a fool to feel disappointed.

Rhys began to put his hose back on. "Orne is usually taciturn, but he can talk for hours about the folly of marriage."

I changed the subject hastily and told the tale the specter had spun. I asked if there really was a ring to extend the dwarf queen's life.

"Yes, but it has power only over dwarfs. It wouldn't help Princess Meryl, and it isn't kept in a chamber under Mulee Forest."

"What would have happened if I'd continued my descent? Would the specter have sealed me in with a boulder?"

He stood and shook his head. "I don't think so. That wouldn't be the specters' way. More likely the tunnel would have looked as it should have for a while, but then it would have branched—"

"And I wouldn't have known which way to go." I pictured it. "I would have turned to call back for advice, and I would have seen more tunnels and no one to . . ." I almost swooned. I took deep breaths and didn't faint.

"Are you all right?"

I nodded and changed the subject again. "Before I came to the Mulee, I defeated an ogre." I told Rhys about it, and the telling made me feel better.

"Your first victory." He bowed to celebrate— exactly as the specter had, which made me shiver.

"Addie . . . Princess Addie . . ."

I shivered again and wondered why Rhys's tongue had slipped. I couldn't imagine that I was "always Addie, simply Addie" in his thoughts too. But if I had let the false sorcerer address me informally, I might as well let the true sorcerer do so. "You may call me Addie, without my title. I don't mind."

He nodded solemnly. "Thank you, Prin— Thank you, Addie." Then he smiled broadly and said, "At the citadel yesterday I worked on something for you, something to impress and astonish you."

It was absurd to feel so pleased.

"May I show you now, to celebrate your triumph over the ogre?"

"Please do." A dragon might fry me tomorrow, and then I'd never know what it was.

Rhys took his baton out of his wide flowered sleeve and pointed it at the sky. He pulled down a small cloud, which he hung over the clearing. "First we need to brighten the Mulee's gloom." He twisted the baton, and the cloud tucked itself into the shape of a crescent moon. He stabbed the air, and the cloud lit up and glowed yellow, the prettiest, most comforting moon I'd ever seen.

"Could I . . . Might I touch it?"

"Go ahead."

I approached the cloud, which obligingly lowered itself. I stretched out my hand, and . . . my finger tingled. I was touching a cloud! "It tingles," I said, patting it. "And it's springy. I like it. It's lovely."

Rhys grinned, looking delighted.

I pushed gently with my finger, and the cloud let me in. Now my whole hand tingled. "Oh!"

After a few moments I withdrew my hand and went to stand next to Rhys.

"Now that we have light . . ." He pulled down another small cloud, an oval that hovered only a few inches above the ground. As I watched, it changed shape and color and became the image of the bench in the old courtyard at home.

Rhys pulled down another cloud. He moved the baton up and down, describing small s shapes and figure eights, and then he pressed the baton in various spots, much as if he were playing the flute.

I gasped. There I was—me as a cloud—seated on the cloud bench.

The cloud me was me at my best—no, beyond my best. The actual Addie had never looked so pretty as this cloud maiden, sitting there in the glow of a cloud moon.

On the cloud Addie my straight brown hair wasn't wispy, was full and graceful instead. My pose—no, her pose was graceful too, her back straight, her long legs tucked under the cloud bench. Her gray eyes were luminous, ardent. She blinked them too often, as I do, which Bella always says makes me look addlepated. But the cloud's blinking only made her look sweet. To my amazement her gaudy green gown became her, brought out the color in her cheeks. She was charming, this cloud Addie.

Another cloud joined me on the bench and

began to take form. I expected it to be Rhys, and it was, except—

"Your chin isn't so long."

"I can never get myself right. That's what I was going to improve before I showed you."

The cloud Rhys stood and bowed. The cloud me curtsied. The cloud Rhys gestured at the sky. The cloud Addie pressed her hands to her heart and nodded.

And then the cloud Rhys picked the cloud me up in his arms and flew her up into the rosy dawn sky!

"Oh!" I said, wishing to be my cloud self.

The cloud moon rose too, and the cloud Rhys and I circled it three times and then set off into the sky, darting here, darting there, entering into the mass of ordinary clouds and reemerging.

The real Rhys at my side waved his baton, and the cloud figures and the moon dissolved into ordinary clouds. Another wave, and the cloud bench rose and merged with its brethren.

"Did you like it?"

"It was glorious!"

He bowed.

If he hadn't told me about Orne's views on marriage, I might have wondered why he'd flown my cloud self in his arms. But now I knew it was only his delight in the dramatic, his pleasure in giving pleasure.

I looked at the sky. It was morning outside the forest, and I had to resume my quest. "Let's leave the Mulee now." I reached into my sack for the magic boots.

"You don't need those. I can fly you out."

Fly me? The real me? In the sky?

"I won't drop you. Flying is . . ."

Hurtling along in my boots was uncomfortable, but I was used to it, and there wasn't far to fall.

". . . the nicest—I can show you how the wind feels, and you can touch more clouds."

He looked so eager. I fought back a hysterical laugh. If he dropped me, at least I wouldn't have to go to a dragon.

"Don't fly me over the moon or around the sun."

"I won't. I promise. Which way are you heading?"

"West."

He lifted me the same way the cloud Rhys had lifted the cloud Addie, one arm under my back, the other under my knees, so I was reclining in his arms. My heart began to hammer—

fear and something else I wouldn't name.

"We'll leave the Mulee the quick way," he said.

The forest floor fell away. A moment later we were sailing above the highest leaves on the tallest trees. Rhys flew vertically, as though standing upright. He wasn't nearly as fleet as my magic boots, but this mode of travel was much sweeter, once I got over my fright. I leaned my head against his chest and was surprised to feel the heat of his skin through his cloak.

"Do you feel my sorcerer's flame?" he said into my hair. "It burns there, just above my breastbone."

"Yes," I murmured. "I feel it."

We passed beyond the forest, but he continued flying for several minutes before lighting on a hillside overlooking a lake. I stood away from him and hoped my heart would stop pounding soon.

He spread his arms wide. "Isn't it fine, Addie?"

I nodded. The lake reflected the sky and was home to two handsome swans. A line of flowering trees, bedecked with pink blossoms, marched up the hill.

"Thank you for setting me down here."

He bowed, reminding me of the specter again.

"I suppose a specter would be able to mimic me as completely as it mimicked you," I said.

"I'm not sure. It wouldn't know whether to be the timid Addie or the Addie who tosses ogres to their fate and orders specters to do her bidding."

I shook my head at the compliment. "I was terrified both times."

"You managed nonetheless." He paused and then said, "I have to leave you in a few minutes. Where are you going next?"

I took a deep breath. "To the desert to find a dragon."

"A dragon!" Rhys was quiet. Then he said, nodding, "You're right. A dragon is Princess Meryl's best hope. But Addie, I don't like . . . I wish I could . . ." He fell silent again for a few moments. "I know something of dragons, more than humans know."

"Please tell me." I sat on the grass.

He crouched next to me. "They're solitary. They dislike other dragons and hate all other creatures. Yet they're lonely and they enjoy conversation. It's why they spin out the deaths of their human victims. If you're captured, you must keep the dragon entertained."

Entertained! I hated talking to strangers. How would I entertain a dragon? "What entertains them?"

"I suppose . . ." His face became still. "They're calling me, and I won't be able to leave again."

"When will it end?"

"The final event is in six days." He added, speaking quickly, "Dragons' bellies aren't their only tender spot. They can be hurt through the undersides of their claws and through their ears." He stood. "Take care. I would hate . . ." He rose into the air.

Hate what?

In a moment he was but a speck, and then he was gone.

I wished he could have stayed. I had never felt so alone. I was the wrong sister for this.

I pulled the spyglass out of my sack. Time to find a dragon. Time to *entertain* a dragon.

Chapter Eighteen

*B*ella had taught us about dragons, and Meryl used to pore over the tomes in Father's library for dragon lore. They were known to hunt for a day or more at a time, preying on horses, cattle, goats, or sheep, and, when the mood struck them, on people. They'd usually gorge on the livestock immediately, and the animals' owners would find the bones. But human bones were never found. And more than once a dragon had been spotted flying with a captive clutched in a coil of its tail. We believed that they toyed with their prisoners, sometimes for months, before killing them. In *Drualt* the hero rescued a maiden after slaying the dragon Yune, and the maiden was witless and half dead from five weeks of torment.

When not hunting, dragons slept a great deal, but they also gloated over their hoards of bones and plunder—weighing, counting, admiring. What else they did I didn't know, whether they recited poetry or sang or whittled chair legs.

I knew one thing more. I knew I'd never defeat a dragon in combat. My only hope lay in tricking it. But how would I trick a creature known for its cunning? I thought about it, and the morning ticked by.

Finally an idea came to me. I'd go to its lair while the dragon was asleep or away hunting. I'd stand still in my seven-league boots—no mistakes, no stumbling—and wait for the dragon to awaken or to return. As soon as it did, I'd say that I expected to die for the knowledge, but would it please tell me the cure for the Gray Death? It would think I couldn't get away, so it might tell me. As soon as it uttered the words, I'd take a step and be gone.

It seemed simple.

I pulled out Rhys's map of the western desert. There were few landmarks—an oasis near the desert's northern border, another in the central desert, and the lairs of three dragons. A lair marked *Kih* was within twenty miles of our western border with the kingdom of Pevir. Another, marked *Jafe*, was southeast of the first, about a hundred miles away. The third was in the central desert, not far from one of the oases. That one was marked *Vollys*, the same Vollys who had swooped down and taken a farmer last year. The same Vollys whom Meryl had hoped to slay.

I raised the spyglass, meaning to direct it toward the desert. But my arm had other ideas and aimed it north, at Bamarre castle. I held my breath and then began to breathe again. The gray pennant did not fly. Meryl was holding her own!

She was in bed, leaning against her pillows and staring out her window. I wondered if she had any hope I'd find the cure.

I lowered my spyglass and set the rings where I guessed Vollys would be. She was believed to be the oldest dragon in Bamarre, and I reasoned that she was more likely than the others to know the cure for the Gray Death.

The desert was a place of huge boulders and low sandstone cliffs. My eyes sought anything living, but the landscape was barren. I kept scanning until I saw smoke curl around a tall boulder. I followed the thread of smoke to a cave in a sandstone cliff. I turned the last ring on the spyglass, and there was Vollys, sleeping in front of her lair.

She wasn't what I expected. She didn't sprawl in slumber. Her wings were tucked in neatly, and she lay curled into herself, with her long head resting on one of her front legs. I had seen the castle cats at home sleep just that way hundreds of times.

While I watched, she opened one eye and looked my way. I felt skewered in her gaze, even though she was too far away to see me. Her eyeball was clear and glittery and faceted as a diamond. Her gaze, cold and clever, was probably directed at a poor desert snake.

But perhaps she did see me. Dragons *knew* things. Perhaps they *saw* things. Perhaps she saw my intentions and my fear and now knew about me and Meryl.

The eye closed, but I no longer had confidence in her sleep. If I went to her, I was convinced, she'd be awake to receive me.

I reset the spyglass to find the dragon Kih. There. The lair, with a jumble of bones piled outside, but no Kih, and no Kih nearby. He was probably away hunting.

I put on my magic boots, although my hands were trembling and I could barely tie the laces. I straightened up and raised the spyglass once more to check my direction.

There was Kih, landing before his lair, wings beating, front legs bearing the bloody carcass of a horse. His snout was stained and dripping red.

I swayed and almost took a step. Weak-kneed, I sat. If he had delayed a few minutes, we would have arrived at the same moment.

I raised the spyglass once again and searched for Jafe.

Another empty lair—no, not empty. A tail extended from the mouth of the cave, and I made out the shadowy shape of the dragon within. The tail thumped the ground, then twitched left to right. Jafe wasn't sound asleep either.

I looked again at Vollys. Both eyes were closed, but one back leg was scratching her side. I didn't dare go to her.

I tried to think of another plan, but I couldn't think of anything, except that I was hungry. So I changed my boots and took out the tablecloth. As I ate, I kept pausing to look in on the dragons. I watched Kih drag the carcass into his lair. Jafe remained inside his cave, and Vollys continued her restless slumber.

I finished my meal. "Good tablecl—"

A shadow moved across the lake. I looked up.

Seven gryphons flew noiselessly toward me. I reached for my magic boots, but it was too late. They were above me, diving at me, cackling and screeching. I pulled Blood-biter from my sack.

I stepped away from the tablecloth so I'd

have room to swing the sword. New dishes began to appear—roasts, loaves of bread, heaping platters—as if to greet new guests.

The gryphons descended on the food. They didn't even glance my way.

They began feeding before their feet even touched the tablecloth. Droplets of gravy spewed into the air, pitchers were overturned, dishes were knocked to the ground and pounced on. The creatures screeched as they ate, and they shoved and pecked each other to reach what they wanted. Sometimes they drew their fellows' blood and supped on it along with everything else.

They stank of sweat and rotting food. Their lions' hides were crisscrossed with oozing welts and black scars, and their eagles' feathers were sparse, with rust-brown skin showing through.

For a few minutes I was too stunned to think. Then I woke up. I didn't know how long the tablecloth could keep producing food, and when it stopped, the gryphons would attack me. I reached for my sack so I could don the magic boots and leave. But as soon as I moved, a gryphon came at me. I drew back from the sack, and it returned to its meal. I tried again, and this time two creatures came at me.

I was to be their dessert. I stood still,

clutching Blood-biter, trying to think of something to do. I was going to die here. Rhys would search for me, and he'd find my skeleton picked clean.

More and more dishes appeared. The gryphons settled down to steady eating and no longer shoved each other or cried out. The afternoon passed. The tablecloth never flagged.

The day was almost done when the first gryphon fell off the tablecloth. The monster wheezed, and its sides heaved. Then it made a gurgling sound and died with its mouth and eyes open. It had gorged itself to death.

Its brethren didn't stop eating, and in the next ten minutes another gryphon fell and died.

In half an hour they were all dead.

I stepped over the bodies to get to the tablecloth, which was piled high with gnawed bones and broken crockery. "Good tablecloth . . ." My voice broke. "Thank you, thank you for saving my life." Two new dishes arrived, a tureen of stew and a chocolate cake. I began again. "Good tablecloth, I thank thee for a fine meal."

The new food and the remains of the old popped out of sight. I patted the tablecloth, folded it, and tucked it into my sack. Then I moved away from the dead monsters. When I was far enough to escape their stench, I took out my spyglass and trained it on the desert.

Vollys had left her lair. This was my chance.

I heard something above me, the beating of wings. More gryphons?

But it was just two vultures, circling overhead, dark shapes against the sunset. Another in the distance was coming to join them.

I turned back to my spyglass. I wanted to see Meryl once more before I left for the desert.

A gray pennant flew from the highest tower.

Chapter Nineteen

I found Meryl's bedchamber. Father was at her bedside, reading from *Homely Truths*. Bella was weeping, and Milton was drawing the curtains closed. For a sickening moment I thought Meryl had already died, but then I saw her fingers on the counterpane curl and uncurl.

It was the sleep. Nine days of sleep, three of fever, and then . . . death.

I lowered the spyglass. I was crying too hard to see.

More vultures had arrived. There were a dozen or more, gobbling and gabbling.

I had to go home. I had to be there, had to touch Meryl, kiss her forehead. I had to cry with Bella, had to ask Milton what he knew. I'd stay only a few minutes. Vollys could wait that long.

I heard squawks and a frenzied beating of wings. I looked around. The birds were leaving, in a great uprush of flapping and feathers. I wondered why. Then I saw—

A dragon, swooping down over the lake, coming this way.

Had it seen me? It wasn't flaming. I reached into my sack for my magic boots.

It landed and wrapped its tail around me so tightly that I could barely draw breath. Its scales were searing hot.

Bells clanged. Deep bells, high bells, light trilling bells. I saw the dragon's face. It was laughing.

I looked away, looked at the sky, at the blossomy trees. My eyes wouldn't focus. Terror kept them sliding past that huge lizard face. I made swimming motions with my arms and shuffled my feet, trying to walk although I was trapped.

The dragon laughed on. Then it spoke. Its voice was metallic and nasal. "I am Vollys. I am so glad to meet you. I meet humans in odd circumstances, and this may be the oddest of all. What is your name, maiden?"

I tried, but I couldn't speak. I coughed, but no words came. I opened my mouth. I shaped the words *I am Princess Adelina*, but no sound emerged.

"I will be disappointed if you do not talk to me, but perhaps you will be more at your ease when I bring you home."

Home! Home to her lair—and me in my ordinary boots.

"Now I hope you will excuse me. I came here to dine. Finding you is an extra treat." The bells of her laughter started again, but shorter and lighter this time. "Watch carefully, love. Dragons are the only beings who can cook their food as they eat it."

She began to drag me toward the gryphon carcasses. I grabbed my sack as I passed it, and she let me.

"Observe. I shall use a hot flame because it is unwise to eat gryphon unless the flesh is well cooked." She breathed in deeply and exhaled a stream of fire.

Smoke burned my throat.

In a few minutes she swallowed her flame. "Cooked to a turn." She stuck her snout into the gryphon and tore into it. Flames licked around her cheek.

When she opened the gryphon's stomach and saw its contents, she turned my way. "Do you mean for me to die of gluttony too? Very clever, setting a trap for them and then using them as a trap for me." She wagged her head. "You intrigue me, little one."

She went back to the carcass. Soon the first gryphon was bare bones. She began on another.

Dusk turned to night while she ate.

Her tail never loosened its grip, and her scales never cooled. I became desperately thirsty.

I tried to think of some way to save myself, but my mind skittered here and there. I remembered my magic boots, but I couldn't put them on, and even if I could, I'd never be able to pull the dragon as I had the ogre. Vollys was as tall and wide as a cottage and three times as long.

The moon rose. The stars came out, and the air turned chill. My head and my toes almost froze, while my torso almost melted. Vollys finished the second gryphon and started on the third. I escaped my fright by falling asleep.

I dreamed of drinking flagon upon flagon of sweet water and being thirsty after every drink. I dreamed of being home in bed, but my legs were under too many blankets. I dreamed of the friend who had repaired my injured arm. He said, "Endure, brave mouse. Your end—"

I was dragged one way and then, sharply, the other.

"Wake up, my dear."

My feet scraped the ground, and my neck almost snapped when she flipped her tail from side to side. I bleated in fear.

"Good. You are awake. I am finished here,

and we can go home. First we will stop at that pretty lake. You will drink your fill, and then I will."

The tail held me awkwardly over the water, sometimes dunking my whole head and sometimes raising me too high to drink. I choked and sputtered and drank.

Steam rose when Vollys lapped up the water. An hour or more passed while she drank half the lake. As she did, I began to be able to think. I might have a chance to escape while she slept off her meal. I could ask her about the cure as soon as we arrived, and then, while she slept, I could slip on my magic boots and depart.

At last she finished. She raised her head and said, "It is my great pleasure, little one, to introduce you to the delights of flying."

She pushed off with her tail. One moment I was upright, and the next I hurtled along sideways, hanging on to my sack with both hands, knowing that if I lost it, I'd lose everything.

The earth and stars swung sickeningly by, and I hung upside down. Only the tail's suffocating grip kept me from falling.

We rose, much higher than Rhys had flown. The lake below shrank to no bigger than a teacup. My stomach heaved, and I retched.

Vomit spilled onto the tail and into the sky. Yet I still kept my hold on the sack.

Then the tail steadied with me upright and remained so for the rest of the journey. Twice Vollys flew over villages. I could make out lamps burning in a few windows. I wept with yearning to be inside a house, in a bed, with nothing more than the wind's whistle to frighten me.

After an eternity Vollys came down in front of the lair I'd seen in my spyglass. She released me, and I stumbled and almost fell.

"Step inside, my dear, where you can warm yourself in front of my cozy fire." She laughed, and those bells clanged again.

I began to run. It was useless, but I didn't think of that. Her tail caught me and deposited me back at the cave's entrance.

"You are being tiresome, little one."

She prodded me with her tail, and I stumbled into the dark cave. The stench almost overcame me. Dragon stench—hot and stale and metallic, so strong and pressing I might have been inside the rock, breathing rock.

Vollys's bulk filled the entrance, extinguishing the moonlight. I backed away from her, stumbled, and fell onto something soft. I jumped up again, afraid of what it might be.

She followed me in. She flamed, and I thought my heart would explode in fright. But it was only a small flame, which she used to light lamps atop several tall torchères.

The lair was beautiful. It was a single chamber, large enough to accommodate three dragons or more, and so high that its ceiling was lost in shadow. By the candleglow I saw that the rock walls were burnished a deep gold. Across from the cave's opening a thin stream of water ran down the rock and collected in a small, shallow pool.

Starting a few feet from the water's edge, the ground was covered with layers of rugs and tapestries. I had fallen back on a pile of velvet cushions. I put my sack down next to the pile. More cushions were scattered here and there. To the right of the pool sat a dozen or more large chests, some open, some shut, and some shut and padlocked. Curio cabinets and two broad wardrobes lined the walls. Except for one, which stood empty, the cabinets were filled with treasure: one entirely with silver stirrup cups, another with jeweled tiaras, and another with weapons—long swords, falchions, poniards, pikes, halberds, maces—some of silver, some of gold.

"Not what you expected, I imagine. One of

my guests was a carpenter." Vollys yawned. "He came as a soldier with a company of his mates, but he remained as my guest and companion, and I discovered what an artist he was." She chuckled, a light clanging. "His remains remain with me to this day.

"Now, little one, you must speak to me. I am beginning to feel slighted."

She waited.

I swallowed. I tried to speak and brought out only a squeak.

"Perhaps you need encouragement." She exhaled a fireball.

Chapter Twenty

My tattered skirts caught fire, and I screamed. Vollys spat and put out the blaze. "Ah, you have a voice."

I bit back another scream. Half my skirts were cinders, through which I saw bright-red skin. My left thigh roared with pain.

"Now speak."

"When will you kill me?"

Vollys wagged her head. "That is not a fit subject for conversation between us. It cannot be very interesting even to you. Come. Suppose you were safe at home, wherever that may be. Even there your life might have only a few more minutes to run."

I held off another yelp of pain.

"But at home would you waste time speculating about your death? You would not. I do not, and I am no more immortal than you are." She yawned again. "Speak of something else."

I couldn't think of anything. I couldn't think of words even. But words came. I blurted out, "What is the cure for the Gray Death?"

Her bells clanged. "A question for a question—what had you to do with the death of seven gryphons?"

I couldn't think what to tell and what to hide. The pain in my thigh was agonizing. "Um . . . nothing. I live nearby."

"You are lying, and so shall I—the cure for the Gray Death is a swallow of milk." She made a clucking sound. "Enough. I am too tired to trade nonsense with you. I hope you will be more sensible when I awaken."

Sleep, I prayed, and let me get away. I gathered up my tattered skirts and tried to cover my naked, scorched thigh.

She went on. "I will sleep, and you may too, but I will sleep longer. If you are hungry, there is food, traveler's fare, in that trunk." She pointed at a chest.

I made myself concentrate on what she was saying, although my mind kept sliding away.

"And you may pick out a gown from this wardrobe." She pointed again. "When I awaken, little one, I suggest you answer my questions candidly, since I will discover the truth anyway. I also suggest that you think of a way to amuse me. It is the only payment I expect for my hospitality."

She began to back out of the cave, and for a

moment I thought she might leave entirely. "Everyone hopes to depart while I sleep, but I always shut the door tight." She placed herself halfway in the cave and halfway out, so that she filled the entrance. She closed her eyes. "I am the door."

I couldn't escape. I lowered myself onto the cushions and huddled there, rocking myself.

Every few minutes one of her eyes would open a slit. I wanted to take out my moily herbs in hopes they would ease my pain, but I didn't want her to see them.

The pain grew so insistent that I had to do something. I limped to the pool at the back of the cave. At least I could bathe my leg. The pool water was warm, but the trickle running down the rock was almost cold. I sat so that the water flowed over my thigh. It helped, but the pain was still terrible.

Eventually my eyes closed, and I escaped again into sleep.

It was a restless slumber. I felt the pain all the while, only slightly muted, and all the while I knew I should be awake—planning, doing, preparing—but I couldn't rouse myself.

Finally I woke up. I stood. The pain returned at full force, and I almost cried out. It was day outside. I could tell because Vollys's back and sides were outlined in light where they touched the lair's entrance.

She was truly asleep. Her eyelids no longer fluttered, and the skin of her cheek sagged over her lip. Her breathing was deep and even.

Just in case, though, I faced away from her to unpin the pouch of moily herb from my shift. I sucked on a flower, and the pain receded, although it crouched a short way off, ready to pounce again. I wondered if the herb would do some good if it touched the burn. I took another flower and pinned the pouch to my shift again. Then I passed the flower gently over my thigh.

Instantly the blisters closed up and shrank away. The skin was still red, but the pain was barely a whisper. Oh, thank you, Milton.

Vollys moaned softly, and I froze. But she just shifted into the pose I had seen in the spyglass. There was her ear hole, below a fold of scales, and there was a patch of pink belly showing a few inches above the ground. Someone more fearless than I could pull out Blood-biter and stab her.

Someone more foolhardy, I realized. A cabinet full of weapons stood in plain sight. She would never sleep if she were in danger. She'd probably be awake the second my hand touched Blood-biter.

I dared to take out my spyglass. Vollys didn't stir. I trained it on Bamarre castle. Meryl was smiling in her sleep, and I hoped her dreams were sweet. She had eight more days of sleep, counting today. Then the fever.

At least I was with a dragon. Perhaps I could persuade Vollys to tell me the cure to the Gray Death, if she knew it. I'd worry about escape once I learned the cure.

I decided to eat something to keep my strength up. I would have liked to use my magic tablecloth, but I didn't know what Vollys would do if she woke and saw it.

I went to the chest she had said held food. A black spider crawled across the lid. It was big, with long probing legs. I stood still, clenching my teeth to keep from screaming.

The spider stopped crawling. It might have seen me. It might be poisonous. It might spring on me.

I told myself that it didn't care about me. It was probably only interested in grubs and flies. I couldn't calm myself, though. Tears streamed down my cheeks.

It began to crawl again. If it crawled away, I would be tormented, knowing it was somewhere, but not knowing where. I had to do something.

It reached the edge of the chest and began to climb down the side. When it got down, it would slip under a carpet and be gone.

I raised my hand to kill it, but I couldn't make myself touch it. I tore a swatch off my ruined skirt. I'd make the spider climb on the cloth, and then I'd carry the horrible creature to the cave entrance and force it to crawl out.

But my hand shook too much.

Then, through my misery, I realized how absurd this was, my terror at a spider with a dragon sleeping nearby. I had to smile, and that steadied me. I balled the cloth and pounded it into the hideous black body.

It was dead. I had killed it.

Now that it was dead, I knew it had meant me no harm. My fear of spiders evaporated. I would try not to destroy an innocent life again.

I opened the chest. Everything was wrapped in damask napkins. Brown crackers were in one and dried meats in another. I ate a few of the crackers, which were stale. I didn't touch the meat. Vollys might consider it a fine joke to feed her current guest a meal of the last one.

I fetched my sack from the pile of cushions. I felt safer when I held it. The seven-league boots were still my best chance of escape.

But what if she went through my sack and found them! I had to hide them. I looked around wildly.

I could put them in the food chest, under the napkins. No, she might rummage in there for food for me.

Another chest? Not an open one. It might be open because she used it often. I went to a closed chest and lifted the lid. It was filled with skulls and bones. I shut the cover quickly.

She could awaken at any second. I spun around, searching with my eyes. The curio cabinets were useless—everything in them was in plain sight. The wardrobes? I ran to one, my steps muffled by the layers of carpet. Yes, I could thrust the boots to the back, behind the gowns. But I hesitated. If she suspected me, Vollys would certainly search the wardrobes.

I stepped away—and noticed something. The rock wall curved, and the back of the wardrobe was straight. There wasn't much room, but there was some. I carried the sack to the wardrobe and stuffed the boots behind it.

They were as safe as I could make them. Now I had to stay alive long enough to use them.

After hiding the boots, I slept too. I woke to worry, mostly about Meryl, but also about how to entertain Vollys and what to tell her of my story. I'd have to tell her something about me. I could tell her about my quest, because I'd already asked about the cure, but I had no idea what else was safe.

Finally I decided to tell the truth, or I'd get tangled in a web of lies, and she would find me out.

I felt calmer after deciding, and all at once I was ravenous. Since I was going to reveal the magic tablecloth anyway, I asked it for a meal. As I ate, my eyes rested idly on the cloth's elaborate embroidery. Then I stared fixedly. Embroidery! Perhaps I had my own way to entertain a dragon.

After I ate, I lifted away layers of rug at my feet till the ground was exposed. Using Bloodbiter, I began to draw by scratching into the packed sand that was the cave's floor. When I was done, I replaced the rugs as carefully as I could. From then on I avoided stepping there.

I established my place within the lair only a few feet away. The spot was near the rock wall and as far as I could be from Vollys. There I set my sack, there I arranged a mound of cushions, and there I ate and slept.

During that first day of Vollys's slumber I bathed in the pool near the back of the cave. Then I chose a gown from the wardrobe she had pointed out to me. If I escaped—*when* I escaped—it would be best if my gown were more than tatters.

Most of the gowns were made for noble-women or royalty. The bodice of one was set with rubies, and the train of another was sprinkled with emeralds. But I wanted more modest attire that wouldn't get in the way if I had to move quickly.

After a long search I found something simple. The tan skirt closed with a wide sash, and the brown bodice had sleeves that ended at my elbows, a blessing in the steamy lair. The skirt and bodice fit me well enough, and when I donned them I felt safer, just because I was dressed.

I often used my spyglass to gaze at Meryl. Her face looked thinner, and I wondered if she was eating anything. I saw Milton raise her up to change her bedclothes, but I never saw him feed her.

For hours I watched, watched her shift from

her side to her stomach and back again, watched her frown in her sleep, watched her smile.

I wished I had never asked her to delay her adventures until I married. It was my fault that she hadn't yet slain a gryphon or fought an ogre. It would be my fault if she never did.

Chapter Twenty-one

Sometimes I used the spyglass to look in on Rhys at the sorcerers' citadel. The first time I did so, I found a hundred or more sorcerers in a vast circular chamber that had no ceiling. It was night, but the stars shone uncommonly bright and illuminated their upturned faces.

Some faces were dark, some light, some male, some female. All were framed by dark, wavy hair and white collars over dark-blue mantles. The sorcerers' arms were all at their sides, palms forward. Their lips all moved as they sang or chanted.

I thought I'd never be able to find Rhys, but then I caught a flash of red. There he was, a rosebud peeking out of his collar.

On one occasion I saw him drift through a garden with another sorcerer, and I wondered if that was Orne, lecturing on the dangers of marriage.

On another occasion I saw Rhys lean over a bowl of water. He blew on it, and it turned cloudy. He blew again, and the water clarified.

He dipped his finger in, stirred once, and a fat orange fish swam in the bowl. He stirred again, and the fish swam through a forest of green plants.

When I was saddest and most frightened, I put the spyglass aside and sought solace by reading *Drualt*. The lamps, which never ran out of oil, provided enough light to read by. The poem's words seemed more powerful here than in my bedchamber at home, for Drualt had been a prisoner too.

It had happened when he was a lad and visited evil King Eldred's court in the kingdom of Tyor. After Eldred failed to kill him by guile, the king threw him into a dungeon deep below Tyor castle.

> *The dungeon walls were stone,*
> *Hard as an ogre's head.*
> *Its floor was dirt,*
> *Soft as milady's powder.*
> *Drualt burrowed,*
> *His belt buckle for a shovel,*
> *Singing all the while,*
> *"Dig or die, dig or die.*
> *Lucky am I to own*
> *A plucky silver buckle."*
> *Drualt the laugher*

Laughed and sang,
"Lucky plucky buckle,
Plucky lucky buckle."
And, laughing more,
"Buckle plucky lucky."
Laughing loud, he sang
Till his tongue
Turned topsy-turvy
And he could sing no more
For laughing.

I wasn't yet brave enough to laugh, but I smiled. As though she sensed my pleasure, Vollys grumbled in her sleep. My smile retreated in fear, but then—

Then I felt a hand on my shoulder, a large hand, imparting cheer and a vast reserve of courage. I whirled around and saw nothing more than the lamplight dancing merrily on the rock walls.

Dancing *merrily?*

The air in the cave shuddered as if in a spasm of laughter. Not Vollys's clanging-bell laughter, but true human laughter, as welcome as sunshine after weeks of rain—as welcome as reaching home after an eternity of danger.

Then the hand was gone, and the laugh ended. The lamplight flickered on the rock walls. It didn't dance. Had Rhys brought me the moment of cheer, or had some happy spirit? I hoped it was Rhys. But whatever the source, I was comforted.

Vollys slept through three of Meryl's eleven remaining days. I was wild with impatience, but still I was afraid to rouse the dragon.

When she finally awoke, I was asleep, sprawled across my pile of cushions. She woke me by blowing a stream of smoke at me, stinking and wickedly hot. I sat up and waved my arms to clear away the smoke. My eyes streamed and my throat burned, and my terror returned.

"Something is different," she said. "You did something while I was asleep. What was it?"

Did she mean the boots? "I d-did nothing." I coughed. "I t-took a gown and—"

"Not the gown. Something else." She sniffed the air and raked the cave with her eyes. "Hmm . . ." She lumbered to the wardrobe the boots were hidden behind and opened it. She shifted the gowns inside. Then she straightened up and closed the doors.

"Little one . . ." She advanced toward me.

I stood and backed away a step.

Her voice sweetened. "We must not quarrel. I

will discover whatever you've done. You needn't confess. I may even be pleased if you've been clever."

She couldn't discover the boots! What would I do?

"It will teach me more about you, which is what I want most." She stopped and sat a little way from me. "Now you must tell me how you came to be on a hillside with a flock of dead gryphons. Tell me, or I will be angry."

I wet my lips, opened them, pushed out air, but no sound.

I saw fire between her teeth, and her tail switched. She breathed in. In a second she'd flame at me.

"You are frightening me." My voice was a raspy whisper. "If . . ." I swallowed. "If . . . if you wish me to talk"—my voice gained strength—"you must not frighten me so much. I can't talk when I think you're about to set me ablaze. But burning me to death will amuse you for only a moment." I was amazed at my bravery. "It will be better for us both if you swallow your flame."

She did! She swallowed the flame, and her bells started clanging again. She was laughing.

I felt so relieved, I even felt safe enough to breathe deeply. With the lair's entry clear, the air was better than any I'd taken in since I was brought here. It was day again.

Sitting up, Vollys reminded me of councillor Lord Tully's pet dachshund. Floppet had short legs too, and when he sat up, they stuck straight out and looked comical, just as Vollys's did— although I was far from laughing.

"I thought you would interest me, little one, and I was right. I shall reward you. Do you see that empty cabinet?" She pointed. "It is yours. You may take something from one of my cabinets and put it in yours. Go ahead. Pick something."

This was peculiar. I gathered my courage again. "If you wish to give me a gift, then tell me the cure for the Gray Death and let me go."

"Perhaps I will. Later. But now you must choose something for your own. You will have your own hoard within mine. It will make you feel at home to have things that belong to you. Now choose." I heard fire crackle in the back of her throat.

I walked from cabinet to cabinet. I hated to imagine in what agony they'd died, the former owners of Vollys's hoard. Some of them must have put great store in their share of this treasure. It made my flesh crawl to think of it.

One object was an ivory carving of a maiden

playing a harp. The harp was made of gold, inset with sapphires. By contrast, the maiden was unadorned, wearing a simple gown and a simple cap. Only her fingers touching the harp were tipped with diamonds. Her expression was rapt—she was joy in music made visible.

Another object was a silver chalice onto which a hunting scene had been etched. In the scene three archers and their barking hounds held an ogre at bay.

A third object was a jade pig with merry amber eyes, a smiling mouth, a barrel belly, and garlands of jewel-encrusted flowers around its neck.

I wanted none of them. My temporary ownership was a sham and an insult to the dead. I picked the plainest thing I found, an empty wooden box inlaid with mother-of-pearl. I moved it to one of the shelves she said were mine. "Thank you."

"An interesting choice, little princess."

I suppose I looked startled, because her bells clanged again.

"Oh, I knew you were royal, or noble at least, when I saw you in that gown. Servants and farmers always choose apparel encrusted with gems. May as well die rich as poor, they think. Now show me what you have in your sack."

What would she do when she saw Blood-biter? My hand trembled as I drew it out.

She did nothing and said nothing. When the sack was empty, she told me to put everything on the shelves of my cabinet. "I hope you will share the bounty of your tablecloth with me."

"Of course."

"Now tell me your tale, and do not lie."

I lost my voice again for a moment, but then I breathed deeply and began. "I am Princess Adelina, but I am called Addie. . . ." I told her about Meryl's illness and my search for the cure for the Gray Death. Vollys asked where the special things in my sack had come from. I said that everything except the maps had been left to Meryl and me by our dead mother. I feared that mentioning Rhys and Bella might endanger them. I said that the maps had come from our library.

"I know the queen died, but your poltroon of a father, King Lionel, still lives. He let you go on this mission? He wants two daughters dead?" The fire was back in her voice. "Do not lie to me, little princess."

"N-no. I ran away. But I left him a note that

I believe convinced him not to try to fetch me back." I told her about *The Book of Homely Truths*. I quoted the saying I'd included in my note, and a few others.

She loved the sayings. Her bells rang on and on when I said, "Poverty means more to the poor than to the rich. Wealth means more to the rich than to the poor." In gratitude, she made me take another gift for my hoard. When I ran out of homilies, she began to invent her own.

"What about this? 'The impetuous man is overtaken by his desires.' It would be a fine Homely Truth, no?"

"Very fine," I said.

She laughed delightedly. "Or 'Food for thought requires a mind with teeth.' What I adore about the best of them is that they almost mean something." She laughed for a minute longer. Then she raised her head and sniffed.

"It comes to me." She continued to sniff. "Now I know what you did while I was asleep." She went to the back of the wardrobe and pulled out the seven-league boots. "No one has ever found such an excellent hiding place before."

She lumbered to the cave entrance, reached above it, and lifted down a ring of keys. She opened her largest chest and locked the boots inside. Then she returned the keys to the ledge above the entrance—about thirty feet above my head.

Chapter Twenty-two

Losing the boots meant the end of me. "You might as well kill me now," I said. I wasn't afraid anymore. I was already dead, although I still breathed.

"Ah, little princess, I'm enjoying myself too much to hurt you." She dreamed up five more Truths and laughed over each one.

When she finally stopped chuckling, she lowered herself onto her belly and extended her neck across the cave until her snout was inches from the hem of my gown. Her eyes were level with my shoulder. I had to meet them, couldn't avoid them. Her gaze was hot and intense.

She spoke in a whisper. "Believe me when I say I want you to stay a long time with me. I am sad when I am alone. My unhappiest hours are after I have destroyed a guest. I have never forgotten any of you. I have remembered my first guest for over seven hundred years. He had a short life breathing the air, but a long life in memory."

I nodded and forced myself not to back away. We stared at each other.

I whispered back, "I believe you."

She looked away from me at last. "I never lie to my guests. Think how silly it would be to lie—as silly as lying to these bones." She gestured at an open chest. "Now tell me how you will entertain me." She picked up a bone, stroked it, and placed it back in the chest.

I stammered, "I c-can't amuse you with talk. B-but perhaps . . . I am a good . . ." I went to the spot where I had drawn on the ground and folded away the rugs. My lines were still there, but faint. I retraced them with my fingers. "I took the liberty . . . While you were sleeping, I—"

"Let me see." She approached.

I backed away, speaking quickly. "I have some skill at embroidery. I thought perhaps I could make an embroidery of you. I have cloth. . . ." I hurried to my cabinet and fetched the wooden ball Rhys had given me. "And there's thread aplenty in the wardrobe if I—"

"Hush." She stared down at my drawing.

In it I had emphasized her grace, the neat lines of her folded wings, her catlike look in slumber. But she might dislike being shown so. She might want a fiercer aspect. Perhaps I should have—

"You portray me sweetly, with a friend's eye." Her voice was soft, calmer than I'd yet heard it. "I should like an embroidery of me exactly thus, surrounded by my hoard." Her voice returned to its ordinary nasal timbre. "And I should like another of me in battle, flaming at a dozen brave knights. We will find cloth for that one too. You have pleased me, little princess. You may take ten things for your hoard."

"Thank you, but I have no need."

"Take them. You will have need. In time I will turn against you, and you will have need."

Before the sun set that day, I embroidered an outline of Vollys onto my cloth, working as slowly as I dared—because how would I entertain her when the job was done? She liked the image and gave me three more things for my "hoard." After that we shared a dinner provided by my tablecloth. I ate a bowl of stew, and Vollys devoured half a roast boar, saying all the while that she didn't usually eat between meals.

If she continued to eat with me, she'd never have to leave her cave to hunt. I wouldn't even be able to try to escape.

The awfulness of it struck me. I'd never be

alone again. I'd be in her dragon presence for every moment of what was left of my life, and Meryl's life too.

After dinner, while Vollys watched, I picked gold threads and purple ones out of a gown. When I was tired, she permitted me to retire to my pillows, but I felt her eye on me and couldn't sleep. I lay rigid for a long while, until at last exhaustion overcame me. My last thought before I fell asleep was that Meryl had only seven more days to live.

When I awoke, Vollys and I shared breakfast from the tablecloth. I had a muffin, and Vollys ate an entire roast lamb. After the meal I sewed while Vollys watched me. She stretched out, with her head less than a yard from me. Her metallic breath heated me almost to melting, and her intent eyes unnerved me. I became terrified of dropping a stitch or adding a color she disliked. It was no way to create. The result was turning out pale and insipid.

I found the courage to say, "Did you oversee the work of your carpenter companion so closely?"

"Yes." She laughed. "He disliked it too."

"Since I am unlikely ever to meet another dragon—"

She laughed more and agreed. "Most unlikely."

"And since I'm unskilled at telling tales, would you tell me of your life? Perhaps you can tell me about the battle you'd like me to embroider."

"Battles are boring, little one." Her tail switched. "I despise being bored. Have you noticed that my eye turns red when I flame?"

I hadn't. I said no, and she sent out a tongue of fire. It was a bit to my right, but the flame still singed my hair and missed my ear by inches.

"I'll warrant you didn't look at my eye then either."

She was right. I said nothing, afraid to admit it.

"I must make allowances. You are my youngest guest but one, and you hardly know me. I will take away only one gift. Give me one of the items in your hoard. You may pick. It is a minor punishment. You'll still have twenty left. You can live for months on twenty. Choose now."

I didn't understand, but I went to my cabinet. I selected a brass goblet, one of the last things I'd chosen, and put it into her outstretched claw. She opened one of her chests, dropped the goblet in, and locked the chest. I wondered why—the goblet hadn't been locked away before.

"Now watch. I shan't hurt you this time. Stand to my side, out of the way, and watch my eye."

I did so. She flamed again, burning nothing, and I succeeded in keeping my gaze on her right eye, the one I could see. It turned orange just before the flaming began, and then it turned wine red. When she stopped flaming, it faded back to orange and then to its diamond translucence.

She blinked twice. "In your embroidery of the battle, my eye must glow. Perhaps you could sew in a ruby. Can you do that?"

I nodded.

"Good. For the battle scene, my skirmish with King Willard will do."

I blinked back sudden tears. King Willard was our bravest king, the king who'd forced a specter to prophesy the cure for the Gray Death. In his thirty-sixth year he had gone off with a company of knights and soldiers to slay monsters, and neither he nor any of his men were ever seen again.

"This is the scene that you will sew: I am swooping low and flaming. Ten archers back away while loosing their arrows at me. Flames dance around their legs. A stallion rears in fright, his mane afire. Three knights run from the fray. You must convey that they are doomed even as they flee. Only one stalwart warrior, King Willard, stands his ground against me."

She lowered her voice to a whisper, "How dear he was, that brave king."

"What became of him?"

She sighed. "I tired of him. He vexed me. One by one he forfeited the gifts in his cabinet. When they were all gone, the last of my love for him was gone too, and he died." Her eyes were moist. "As soon as he was gone, I loved him again and missed him dreadfully. As I shall love and miss you someday."

Chapter Twenty-three

Vollys sat up, and her gaze left me at last. She began to tell me about King Willard and some of her other "guests." I wondered if any of them had tried to escape and if any had succeeded.

She smiled at a memory. "Willard would rail at me for stealing his subjects' livestock. But I'd say I was only collecting his taxes for him, since the cattle, a portion of them anyway, were destined for his royal stomach. Oh, I loved to match my wit against his."

She also loved to watch him cook his meals, an exacting process, because he was fastidious. She told me this over lunch from my magic tablecloth.

"You are fastidious too, but some of my guests, little princess, are not fastidious in the slightest. I remember one man, a duke, ripping into the raw leg of a fawn with his teeth. He was not . . ."

I made myself think of other things. I remembered the view from my castle window. I pictured Rhys bowing, Meryl's mock swordplay before she got sick, her indignation . . .

If she were here, she wouldn't ignore a single word spoken by a dragon. I went back to listening. Vollys had returned to her catalogue of King Willard's virtues. His laugh was hearty, he told a tale well, his figure was fine, his beard was curly.

When she paused for breath, I said, "He seems perfect. Why did you tire of him?"

She yawned. "Even perfection becomes tiresome. He was always brave, always courteous, always kind. I began to wonder if he was stupid. The thought tormented me, that I had spent nine months cosseting a stupid man, and two days later I slew him."

"Has anyone stayed beyond nine months?"

Would she be angry if I took out my spyglass to look at Meryl?

"No one. Why are you fidgeting? Am I boring you?" She flicked her tail, and her eyes glowed orange.

I gulped. "Bored? I have reason to be interested in the fate of my predecessors."

The glow faded. She was mollified.

I risked angering her again. "My thoughts often turn to my sister. I cannot help myself." I asked if I could look through the spyglass.

"Certainly, and I will look too."

Those evil, bloodshot eyes, staring at Meryl, appraising her. She couldn't! "Don't! You can't!" I rushed to the spyglass, picked it up, and held it close.

Vollys laughed. "I can, Princess Adelina. I will look in it often someday. But for now, you may use it first."

Meryl's face was pale and worn. I didn't want Vollys to see her this way. I didn't want Vollys to see her at all, but she took the spyglass after only a minute or two.

"Usually she's very pretty," I said.

Vollys held the spyglass up to her left eye. "I can see that. She is lovely, very different from you. Oh, my clumsy tongue." Vollys's bells clanged. "You are lovely too, but in a quieter way. In temperament I see that you are different as well. She could lead a charge, but you could last a siege. This is fascinating, little Adelina. The more I look at her, the more clearly I see you. You may be a worthier opponent than even my Willard was."

She was wrong! I was nothing compared to Meryl. Meryl would have slain her by now. Meryl would be laughing over her bones by now.

"You were great friends, you and your sister. Her name is Meryl, yes?"

I nodded.

"Princess Meryl took care of you, didn't she? You needn't answer. I already know. This is dreadfully sad. She is dying, and you are dying."

Enough!

"I think I must do something. I shall tell you the cure for the Gray Death."

What?

"I will not set you free, but I will tell you. Bring me those maps of yours. I want the one of the Eskerns."

I ran and fetched them. Fumble fingered from excitement and nerves, I dropped the stack at Vollys's feet.

She laughed. "Oh, this is fun. It's so nice to have a guest. Find the right one, child, and give it to me."

I found it, and she lifted it close to her eyes. "Now where is the valley? Whoever made this map did not want it to be read. These lines were drawn by mice. I need better light. Come, carry the map outside, and I will tell you what you want to know." She lowered herself onto four legs and left the cave.

I followed. If she still couldn't read the map, perhaps I could darken the lines somehow.

Leaving the cave, Vollys spread her wings a bit for balance. The pose reminded me of a woman raising her skirts to navigate a puddle.

She stopped a few feet from the boulder that stood outside the cave. "Now give me the map." She sat and held out one front claw.

I did so. How marvelous to be outdoors! There was a light breeze. High above I saw a bird.

"Ah. Much better. Hmm . . . Yes! That's it." She dropped down on all fours again so that half her claw rested on the precious map. It could tear! I began to reach for it and then stopped myself.

"Take it." She raised her leg. "I would not destroy your map. I am not in that sort of mood."

I snatched it away and smoothed it out.

She lay down before me. "Humans are not the only poets and not the only ones to fashion tales to tell their truths. Dragons tell our own tales, and our truths are not the same as yours.

"Have I told you yet who Yune was?"

I shook my head.

"I thought not. Well, before Drualt murdered her, she was my mother."

How old was Vollys?

"I shall declaim for you." She sat up and recited in ringing tones,

> "Swift-flying Hothi,
> Slain by Drualt.
> And Zira, flame
> Of fury, young beauty,
> Her he slew also.
> Men call him
> The Laugher, the Hero.
> Drualt, stifling fire,
> Snuffing life,
> No hero to dragons."

Drualt wasn't cruel! He was kinder than anyone, and no hero to dragons made him a thousand times a hero to us. But it was odd to hear the dragons' version, like discovering what a wild boar thinks about its hunters.

"Hothi and Zira died slow, dreadful deaths." Vollys's voice regained its usual metallic quality. "I was a mere nestling then, but I was shocked. We dragons may fight among ourselves—I admit to liking few of my fellows, perhaps none—but we are clannish. Mother sought revenge against Drualt. Now I shall recite about her."

I wished she would just tell me the cure.

She began,

> *"Yune, the Sly One,*
> *The Enduring,*
> *Yearned to set Drualt's*
> *Sea-green eyes*
> *Atop her treasure hoard.*
> *So she found him*
> *And bore him*
> *Over the peaks,*
> *Across the plains*
> *To her sweet lair. Eagerly*
> *She carried death*
> *To her home.*

"The verses go on, Princess Adelina, but they are long in the telling, and you are anxious to learn the cure."

I was!

"I will summarize. Mother made a single mistake in her battle with Drualt, but she made it again and again. Many times she could have killed him, but she wanted him to die gradually, as Hothi and Zira had. So she only wounded him, scorched his scalp, melted the armor on his chest."

I ached for poor Drualt.

"He gave Mother no such quarter. He struck, when he could, with all his might, and by the time he cravenly hid in her hoard, her belly was scored in a dozen places. As soon as he desecrated her hoard, though, she wanted to finish him. But, as you know, she was loath to flame at her treasures.

> "Yune burned hot and bright
> As the first forge
> That made her. She
> Would have consumed
> Man's hero then, reduced him
> To a speck of soot,
> A splinter of bone,
> But for his treachery.
> From her dear hoard
> He raised against her
> Her own sword taken fairly
> (An age ago) from
> Arkule's dead fingers.
> Drualt thrust the stolen blade
> Through Yune's ancient
> And loyal heart.
>
> "Yune's fire doused,
> Her life fell away.
> Yet still she held
> A bequest, a death gift
> For her enemies. From her belly,
> Roiling with noxious smoke,

> *She belched forth*
> *Contagion, a gray death . . ."*

The Gray Death hadn't swept in from the sea, as some believed. It wasn't a judgment on us for all the wrongs that men commit, as others thought. It had come from Yune!

Vollys went on:

> *"And with a long labored breath,*
> *Yune blew her legacy*
> *To the halls of men.*
> *She sang in a thin thread*
> *Of voice, 'Some will be spared,*
> *Some will be chosen. The chosen*
> *Will die, the spared*
> *Will live and mourn,*
> *Heartsick, their lost loves.'*
> *Then her voice guttered out,*
> *And she succumbed,*
> *Dying avenged, dying glad.*
> *Yune, the Sly One,*
> *The Enduring, flamed no more."*

Vollys bowed her head.

Don't stop now. What about the cure? Recite the stanza about the cure.

"It did not suit us to include the cure in the

story, but there is one." Vollys raised her head. "I was only a nestling then, but Mother whispered it to me before she died."

"What is it?" My voice was soft, but I wanted to scream.

She considered me. "I liked you better before I began to recite. Mother would be alive today if not for humans. Perhaps I shan't tell you after all."

Chapter Twenty-four

I f I could have, I would have shaken her until her bones rattled. Instead, I tried to persuade her. "Won't my death taste sweeter if I know the cure and still can't save my sister?"

"You have completely failed to understand me. Your death will not taste sweet. I will be mourning you even as you lie dying. But it is nice of you to consider my pleasure." Her tone was ironic. "However, you will hasten your death if I tell you. I will be uneasy that you know, which will make me irritable."

She was irritable now. Her eyes were copper colored, and fire coarsened her voice. "Already I have decided to take away two items in your hoard. If I reveal the cure, you will lose two more, equal perhaps to a week of life. Are you willing to make the sacrifice just for the satisfaction of knowing?"

I nodded, although I was frightened. But she couldn't see the future. Something unexpected might happen.

"Very well. Do you see the Aisnan Valley?"

She pointed to a spot on the map with her claw.

The valley lay between the Eskerns' tallest mountains. The map showed more ogre camps on their slopes and more gryphon nests on the peaks than anywhere else in the range. Surprisingly, a village of humans wasn't far away. It was Surmic, the village that hadn't helped Drualt's sweetheart, Freya, when she was attacked by gryphons.

"The valley is irrigated by a high waterfall," Vollys continued. "The water appears to come from the mountain above, but it does not. Instead, it descends directly from the fairies' Mount Ziriat. When the water reaches the earth, it disappears into the ground and surfaces nowhere else. A sip of that enchanted water will cure the Gray Death, but only if the sufferer drinks it there. You cannot collect the water in a flask and bring it to your sister, because it will have lost its power.

"And now you must give me four items from your hoard."

Three more days passed, for Meryl the last days before the fever. For me days of torment—knowing the cure and able to do nothing.

Although she'd taken things from me when she told me the cure, at first Vollys didn't seem angry at me for knowing. On the contrary, I was in high favor. She said she "adored" my embroidery, and she kept showering me with gifts, many more than she'd taken away, until I had seventy-five items in my cabinet.

But then the fourth day dawned, the day Meryl's fever would begin, her three days of fever before the end.

I reached for the spyglass as soon as I sat up, just as I had the morning before and the morning before that. Vollys was watching me as she always did. Before I could raise the glass to my eyes, she said, "I tire of your devotion to your sister." Her voice was husky with fire. "Give me the spyglass. We shan't look at her again." She plucked it out of my hand before I could protest, and locked it in the same chest that held my seven-league boots.

I begged her to give the spyglass back. I swore to ask her permission before looking in it, but nothing I said had any effect. She told me to work on my embroidery. I did, although my vision was blurred by tears.

Now my sewing didn't satisfy her. She complained that the colors I chose were wrong, that I worked too slowly, that I wasn't careful enough. During the morning I had to give back twenty items from my cabinet. Fifty-five were left, which would not last long if she kept taking them twenty at a stroke.

She was restless as well as irritable. She started stories and broke them off. She began to count the bones in a chest and stopped abruptly, leaving a heap on the carpet. She rushed outside and flapped her wings and rushed back in.

In the afternoon she took thirty more items, including Blood-biter, *Drualt*, and my magic cloak. At this rate she'd kill me before nightfall.

At dinnertime she took the magic tablecloth from me. "I shall speak to it from now on." She placed it on the ground. "Good tablecloth, set thyself please."

It did nothing. She repeated the words in a furious whisper. Her eyes glowed red. I was terrified, and I wished the tablecloth would open. She shouted the words, glaring at it. She shouted again, and this time she said the words in their proper order. The tablecloth opened and began to set itself.

"That's better." Her eyes quieted from red to gold. "But I've changed my mind. I don't want to eat now. Good tablecloth, I thank thee for the fine meal."

It finished setting itself and food began to appear.

"Good tablecloth, you will do well to heed me. Good tablecloth, I thank thee for the fine meal."

Say it right, I prayed. Say *a* fine meal.

"You will regret this." A tongue of flame licked a corner of the tablecloth.

Nothing happened. It wasn't even singed.

"Good tablecloth," I began. "I thank—"

She turned on me. Her eyes were bright orange. "I said *I* would command the tablecloth." She roared at it, "Good tablecloth, I thank thee for the fine meal."

Food continued to arrive.

She yelled, "Stop!" and spit a fireball at the tablecloth.

It didn't burn, but the food did. The soup boiled, a loaf of bread turned black, and fire crackled over a roast turkey. The rugs beneath the tablecloth caught fire.

Vollys shrieked. Her tail flailed about, sending chests careening about the floor. She blocked the cave's entrance, so I backed away, hoping not to draw her notice, praying not to be crushed or burned by accident.

The fire in the rugs began to spread toward the rear of the lair, where I stood pressed against the cave wall. Vollys flamed again. An inferno engulfed the tablecloth, reducing the food to ashes, but the cloth still didn't burn. I wished it would. Perhaps that would satisfy her.

Several chests were in flame. A cabinet only a few feet from me caught fire. At any moment my gown would catch.

Vollys strode about the cave, the tablecloth in her mouth. She was biting it and flaming at the same time.

The lair's entrance was clear. I ran toward it. A fiery chest lay between me and my goal. I raced around it. I stepped on burning carpet and kept running.

It was dusk outside. The sole of my right boot was scorched, and my foot smarted. I ran around the boulder outside the lair. I glanced back to see if Vollys was coming after me. She wasn't. I still saw her dark shape in the incandescent cave.

I ran on. I didn't look back again. If she was coming for me, I'd know soon enough.

My throat was parched. The desert map had shown an oasis eight miles away. I would go there and find a place to hide.

I ran.

The moon rose. My breath gave out. I slowed to a walk and allowed myself to look back. I didn't see the lair. I couldn't even tell which cliff it was in.

I slipped from the shadow of one cliff to the shadow of another, hoping I was headed the right way. When my breath returned, I ran again.

Meryl must be awake with the fever by now, I thought. I'd never reach her in time, even if I managed to leave the desert alive. I wouldn't be with her when she died.

I felt a wind, and Vollys landed before me, blocking my way. She flamed at me, and I jumped back, unharmed.

Her bells chimed. "Ah, little Adelina, I've found you. The fire is out, and you may come home." Her tail picked me up, and she returned me to the cave.

The fire was out, but the cave was as hot as an oven. The first thing I saw was a mountain of food rising from the tablecloth, which still hung in the air. Dishes continued to appear, but slowly and in small quantities. Some had fallen onto the carpet, which still smoked here and there.

"Tell that thing to stop, there's a dear."

"Let me go and I'll—"

Vollys's bells clanged. "Little one, I shan't ever let you go if you threaten me. I can find other lairs if your tablecloth is determined to produce meals forever. But I would be grateful if you would save me the trouble."

I would gain nothing by refusing. "Good tablecloth, I thank thee for a fine meal."

The tablecloth stopped serving, and the mess of food vanished. The tablecloth folded itself and hung in the air.

"Take it, little princess. It will feed you while I'm gone."

Gone?

"I could not understand why I was so irritable today. But as soon as I flamed at your tablecloth, I knew. That tablecloth had kept me from hunting, but I must hunt. I'm a dragon. So now, Adelina, I shall do so." She lit the torchères that were still standing and waddled out of the cave.

She was leaving!

I followed her out and stood leaning against the boulder, hoping . . . hoping. . . .

She turned. "I know you mean only to see me off, but I'll just imagine your fond farewell." Her bells rang again. Her tail picked me up and put me back in the cave.

I beat at the tail with my fists, and her laughter grew louder.

"Little princess, I would miss you far too much to let you go." She pushed the boulder to block the cave's entrance.

I was entombed.

Chapter Twenty-five

A mouse could have squeezed through and escaped, but I couldn't. I ran at the boulder and kicked it, only succeeding in making my toe ache.

The cave was in chaos. The wardrobe from which I had selected my gown lay on the floor, its contents ashes. Chests were scattered here and there, some on their sides, some upside down, the wood of many charred and burned, their contents spilling onto the floor.

I sat on a chest that was only slightly charred. Then I jumped up. Where was the big one, the chest with the seven-league boots and my spyglass? I tore through the cave, praying that the boots weren't cinders and the spyglass hadn't melted. I found the chest, on its side and half submerged in the pool at the back of the lair.

It wasn't much burned. A few of the wooden slats were scorched, and one was loose. I scraped my hands trying and failing to pry it off. I rushed to the weapons cabinet, which listed to one side but still stood. I snatched up a sword and raced back to the chest. In a moment I pried the slat free.

But only my hand and forearm fit through. I felt one boot, but the space wasn't big enough to get it out.

I pushed the chest over and saw that the wood around the hinges had been softened by heat and water. It took only a few minutes to chop and dig around them.

I opened the chest and grabbed the spyglass.

Meryl was awake, sitting in the red chair, which was drawn up to the fireplace. She was wrapped in blankets, and the fire was blazing, but her jaw trembled, and I realized that her teeth were chattering. Her eyes were open, shining brightly, too brightly. Her cheeks had turned ashy, the color of the Gray Death.

Milton placed a compress on her forehead. Bella bustled into the chamber with another blanket. Meryl's lips moved. Bella answered her, and then Milton said something. Meryl laughed—my Meryl, laughing in the face of the Gray Death. Meryl, the laugher.

Couldn't I do *anything*? I wished for Rhys. I could tell him the cure, and he could fly Meryl to the waterfall.

Suppose I was ready when Vollys returned. She could return before Meryl . . . She had to!

She would move the boulder aside, and for a moment the entrance would be clear. In that moment I could take a step in the magic boots, and I'd be off to Meryl, to carry her myself to the Aisnan Valley.

I pulled the boots out of the chest. They hadn't burned—they were just damp. I sat on the chest to put them on. There. I stood up— and sat down again. I had to be careful. If I took a step, I would crash into the cave walls or into the boulder, and I'd be dashed to death.

I sat there, thinking. How much time did I have? How much time did Meryl have? If her fever had struck a few minutes ago, she had three days yet to live. But if it had struck this morning, she had little more than two. If Vollys returned tomorrow . . .

There were too many *ifs*. I couldn't plan. I could only be ready. On my knees (because of the boots) I began to search for the other things that had been in my sack. I found Blood-biter, *Drualt*, and my embroidery. It was too dim in the cave for me to see my magic cloak, but luckily my hand brushed against it in the chest that had held Blood-biter. I failed to find the sack itself and the maps, which might have burned up.

It didn't matter about the maps. The location of the Aisnan Valley was etched in my mind.

Except for Blood-biter, I tied everything into a bundle, using the skirt from a lady's gown. If my scheme failed, I would stab Vollys before she killed me. She wouldn't make a pet of me again.

I stood and raised the sword. I slashed the air with it. I began to lunge—

And *something* crashed into me and toppled me. I tried to stand, but it wouldn't let me. I struggled against it, but it was too strong and kept pressing me to the ground. Finally I gave up. Had Vollys left something behind to harry me? I sat back, panting.

Then I realized—whatever had pushed me had saved me. If I had lunged, the boots would have thought I'd taken a step.

"Thank you," I whispered.

In answer, I felt myself lifted into a kneeling position. The sword came up, and I thrust with a strength I didn't know I had. While I thrust, I felt happy—no, joyous.

Vollys didn't return that night or the next morning. I nearly went mad with impatience. I couldn't be still. I crawled about the cave. I cried. I shouted.

Sometimes I read from *Drualt* and wished

for impossible things, things that happened only to heroes in fables.

Sometimes I even worked on my embroidery of Vollys and enjoyed pricking holes in her with my needle.

Sometimes I thought about Rhys. I loved him. If I died here, he'd never know, which might be for the best. If he ever discovered how I longed for him, he'd be miserable.

Most often I looked in the spyglass.

I looked at Meryl, shivering under all her blankets. She ate nothing, drank only a few sips of broth. She was so sick, and her expression was so untroubled. She had such courage!

Once, while I looked, Father entered the sickroom. He stayed five minutes and then left after reading from *Homely Truths*, after staring down at his feet, after speaking to Milton and Bella, after not kissing his daughter, after not shedding a tear.

She laughed when the door closed behind him, and I cried my heart out.

Then I directed the spyglass here and there in Bamarre, beautiful Bamarre. I saw a grove of pear trees near Lake Orrinic, a field of corn in the Bamarrian Plains, fish jumping in a stream in the Kilket range.

In the town of Wempuc I saw a cobbler

finish making a pair of round-toed shoes fit for a duke. Back in the Kilkets I watched goats graze, tended by a sleepy goatherd lad nodding in the shade of a spruce tree.

I was about to lower the spyglass when I saw an ogre lumber down from a higher slope. The goatherd jumped up and fitted an arrow to his bow. The arrow missed its mark, and the boy threw down the bow and raced off down the mountain. Laughing, the ogre ran a few clumsy steps after him before turning back and snatching up half a dozen goats from the bleating, milling flock.

Then my eyes followed the goatherd to his walled village. He dashed through the gate, and someone closed it behind him. A few moments later archers manned the wall, but no one left the village to chase the ogre away.

I peered behind the wall and saw a dozen or more humble cottages, built of wood and thatch. But the village wall was made of stone and very high.

I spent a long while peering through the spyglass. I saw splendid landscapes and I saw people at their work, appearing serene, appearing well fed. But I saw more to dismay me than just one ogre at a flock of goats.

I saw a gryphon swoop down and snatch a baby from its cradle. I saw a troop of ogres besieging a walled town. I saw a coach rolling down a quiet lane, accompanied by a company of archers—and I realized that without the archers, the coach would have had to stay home.

I saw Vollys gorging on a herd of cows in a sea of blazing grass. A castle stood on a nearby hill.

I saw more victims of the Gray Death, young and old, peasants and townfolk and nobles. And I saw the grief of the people who loved them.

For the first time I understood Meryl's zeal to save Bamarre. Father had done little for our subjects, but if she lived, she would bring them relief. I swore that if I lived, I'd no longer stand in her way. I would go with her and fight at her side. If I lived and she died, I would do my best alone.

I put down the spyglass and a few minutes later fell asleep, although I'd sworn not to. When I awoke, it was dawn of the next day, Meryl's last day. I raised the spyglass.

She was up again, sitting as close as she could to the fireplace. Rhys was with her. His ceremony must have ended. He was using his baton to call a cloud into the room. It drifted in and covered Meryl and her chair, making a cloud blanket.

Thank you, Rhys, my love. That will make Meryl warm, if anything can.

I heard a rustle and a thump outside the cave. I rammed the spyglass into my bundle.

"Little princess, stand back. I know you're wearing those boots of yours, but I shan't let you go."

I heard a *whoosh*, and the boulder was lined with flames. On my knees I scrambled to the pool at the back of the cave and rolled in the water till my gown was soaked. Then I stood and waited, Blood-biter drawn. If Vollys flamed at me, I'd hurl the sword. With luck, my dying would bring her pain.

She pushed the boulder aside and left behind a wall of flame. This was my chance, and now that it had come, I felt no fear. I inhaled deeply, raised Blood-biter, lifted my right foot in the magic boots, and took a step.

Chapter Twenty-six

Searing heat! Then I was through. Ahead of me was Vollys, standing upright. I slammed into her, the force of my step driving Blood-biter deep into her belly.

She shrieked.

I thought that my chest had caved in, that my lungs were crushed.

My boots pulled me around her. I would have lost Blood-biter but for my viselike grip on the hilt. After that I remember little. The boots dragged me, bouncing and bumping across the desert, over cliffs, into gullies, while I fought for breath.

Finally the boots slowed and stopped. I lay in a heap, swallowing air in tiny sips, wishing never to move again.

But I wasn't allowed to rest. That invisible *something*—that meddling helper—pushed me, tugged me, wouldn't let me be. *All right!* I thought. I moved my left leg in the beginning of a step, and I was off again.

I was bullied into taking four more steps,

until I was out of the desert and onto the plains. Then I fell, and the spirit let me stay where I was. I lost consciousness.

Meryl! I awoke. I fumbled to unpin the pouch from my shift, fumbled to open it, fumbled to pull out a flower. As soon as it was in my mouth, my mind cleared. For a second I felt the pain at full power, giant hands squeezing my chest. But then the hands loosened their grip, and I breathed easier.

I looked around. I was in a field of tall grass. The sky was cloudy, and a strong wind sent ripples through the reeds. My bundle was next to me. Miraculously it hadn't opened and spilled all my things. I began to reach into it for the spyglass when I saw Blood-biter a few feet away, its blade matted with sand and mud. I took a handful of grass to wipe it clean and saw, beneath the dirt, that it was smeared from tip to hilt with sticky, crimson dragon blood.

Good! I'd be glad if she was dead, glad if Bamarre was rid of her. I looked through my spyglass. She was sprawled before her cave, facing away from me. I watched for several minutes, but I couldn't tell if she still breathed.

I turned the spyglass to find my way home.

Mountains, too low to be the Eskerns, must

be the Kilkets. So Bamarre castle should be—

"Addie! I was looking for . . . Are you hurt?"

Rhys! I began to jump up, but my ribs hurt and I remembered the boots. I sat down again with a thump.

He landed before me. "You're hurt!"

"I'll be all right. I just knocked into a dragon."

He grinned and then bowed. "Is *it* all right?"

"I don't know. Oh, Rhys, I found out the cure for the Gray Death!" I told him quickly. When I got to the part about stabbing Vollys and escaping, he bowed again.

"You and Drualt," he said admiringly, "the only ones to fight dragons and live to tell the tale. I don't think even Drualt ever escaped from one of their lairs."

I wished Rhys could always look at me the way he was now.

"I was on my way home," I said. "I was finding my bearings when you—"

"I can fly you home."

I shook my head. "My boots are faster."

"Might I wear one of them?"

He did, and we held hands so as not to be separated. Rhys skimmed along a few inches above the ground, while I bumped and bounced as usual.

The boots took us within five miles of the castle, and Rhys flew me the rest of the way. As we flew, he shouted over the wind, "I was right. Orne never married. He said your specter must have been a beginner to make up such a thing."

I couldn't think about that now. I was going home, Meryl was still alive, and I was going to save her.

I asked Rhys if he'd been the spirit that had helped me through my adventures.

"No," he shouted back. "I don't know how to be a spirit. I don't think sorcerers can be."

Then who or what had helped me? I offered the spirit a silent thanks. The wind whooshed by without answer or acknowledgment, and we rushed on to Meryl.

She opened her arms, and I ran into them. "I found the cure," I said into her shoulder.

She hugged me with a fevered strength, so hard that my chest hurt again. "Addie, Addie, I'm glad you're back." She sounded hoarse. Her lips were chalky, and her cheeks were dry and flaking. "Look!" She let go of me and stood. "Sir Gray Death has returned my strength to me, for a short while anyway." She shivered and sat in the red chair again, drawing Rhys's cloud blanket around her.

That was good. If she was strong, the trip to the Aisnan Valley would be easier on her.

"I found the cure," I repeated. I hugged Bella and Milton. "The dragon Vollys told me." I explained quickly.

"I wish I could have seen you stab a dragon." Meryl paused. "I wish I could have stabbed her."

Bella said, "The two of you can't go into the Eskerns in the middle of a thousand monsters."

Meryl coughed for a full minute while we waited. "I'll go alone," she said finally. "Addie, give me the boots."

"The trip is too rough," I said. "I'll take you. I'm used to it."

"I'll carry Princess Meryl to the waterfall," Rhys said. "No one else is needed."

"I'm going," I said, hugging my bundle with the boots inside.

"Then I'll wear just one boot," Rhys said.

"Addie will carry me, and I'll carry Blood-biter!" Meryl pointed at it, protruding from my bundle. "I'm strong enough to fight." She coughed so hard, my own throat felt raw.

We all argued for five minutes. Rhys kept

bowing and repeating all the ways he could help us—by commanding the clouds, by fighting gryphons or dragons in the sky, and by moving quickly even without the magic boots. Bella and Milton said they wanted to come too, and Bella kept saying Meryl was too sick to fight. And Meryl kept arguing and coughing while her life ticked away.

I had to do something. I interrupted, "That's enough!"

They all turned to me, looking startled.

"Rhys and Meryl and I will go." I didn't want to endanger him, but he could do things I couldn't. Bella and Milton weren't warriors, and they would slow us down. "Rhys and I will need swords. Meryl will wield Blood-biter." I handed it to her. I wouldn't stop her ever again.

"Hooray!" She buckled on the sword. "Addie's taking charge!"

I kissed her cheek, which felt very hot. "Milton, please ask a servant to fetch swords for Rhys and me."

I went to my bundle to get the spyglass. "I want to see how close we can come to the Aisnan Valley." I remembered the map well enough to work it out.

Everyone was quiet while I looked in the spyglass and calculated.

Finally I said, "The closest we can get is Surmic village, three miles away. We'll stop there and ask the villagers to tell us the best route."

"Surmic!" Bella said. "They won't help you, those treacherous cowards."

"It's only for directions," Rhys said. "Surely—"

"I'm the king's daughter," I said. "I'll command them to tell us." If they refused, I'd rip the words out of their throats.

Milton returned with a manservant, who was carrying two clanking swords. Rhys and I buckled them on.

I asked Milton when the fever had struck Meryl.

"Three days ago."

Meryl grinned. "Sir Gray Death will be surprised when he finds me cured. He intends to carry me off tomorrow at dawn."

Dawn! I was hoping for more time, until midmorning at least. Outside, the day was fading. She had only one night left.

I went to my bundle. "Here's a magic cloak, Meryl. Put it on when we reach the valley." No matter how strong she felt, she had to be weaker than Rhys and I were. "The gryphons and ogres won't see you, and they won't attack while you run to the falls."

"If they attack, I'll fight." But she took the cloak.

The door opened again, and Father came in.

"Daughter . . . Addie. You've returned to bid your sister farewell."

I turned to keep him from seeing my sword. "Greetings, Father."

Meryl pulled the cloud blanket to hide hers. Rhys bowed and concealed his under his cloak.

But Father had noticed. "A tournament in a bedchamber?"

Rhys and I both began to answer. He said, "Sorcerers use swords—" I said, "We were comparing—"

"What is this about?"

Meryl went to her bedside table, the cloud blanket moving with her. She picked up her copy of *Homely Truths*. "Addie has found the cure for the Gray Death." She coughed. "It's a waterfall in the Eskerns. We're going there—we have a way to travel quickly, and the swords are for slaying monsters."

Father turned to me. "How did you discover the cure?"

"A dragon told me." I related what Vollys had said, hating the waste of time. My chest began to hurt again.

When I finished, Father said, "How do I know the dragon spoke the truth?" He sounded indignant.

It hadn't occurred to me that Vollys might have lied.

"It's my only chance," Meryl said, carrying *Homely Truths* back to her chair.

"I know that, Daughter. Nevertheless, I must deliberate. A king must not act precipitously."

"Listen . . ." Meryl held up *Homely Truths*. "'A skirmish avoided is a battle in the making.' We'll—"

"You can follow us with an army," I said.

Meryl turned to a new page. "'The wily serpent strikes twice.' That"—she broke off to cough—"would be you, Father."

"I don't recall that adage."

Rhys said, "Sire, we can strike first and nip the monsters. You can strike next and vanquish them."

Father nodded slowly. "I can follow with an army. Just so. We'll be ready in a week. . . ."

A week! And another three weeks for travel at Father's slow pace.

He patted Meryl's shoulder. "I must go. Never tarry—"

"Farewell, Father." She took his hand and then released it.

He stared at his hand for a moment before lowering it. "Farewell." He smiled awkwardly and left.

The castle bell tolled nine o'clock. We said good-bye to Bella and Milton and left Meryl's chamber. She strode next to me, walking easily, not even stopping when she coughed.

My bundle was tied in a makeshift sling so my hands were free. As well as my boots, the bundle still held the magic tablecloth and my spyglass.

A full moon presided over a starry sky that was dotted here and there with clouds, still pink from the sunset. In the castle garden Rhys and I put on the boots, one apiece. I consulted the spyglass while he lifted Meryl. Then he took my hand, and we stepped.

Chapter Twenty-seven

$\mathcal{T}$he chill night air and the rushing wind made Meryl's fever worse. By the time we reached Surmic village, her teeth were chattering, and I suspected she was shivering under the cloud blanket.

Surmic stood midway up a steep slope. We arrived a few yards from the village wall and exchanged our magic boots for ordinary ones.

Rhys banged on the gate and bellowed, "Halloo there! Let us in."

I shouted, "We come from the king."

Nothing happened.

Rhys said, "I'll fly up and open the gate."

But before he could, a hand holding a lantern appeared at the top of the wall. Someone peered down at us, and a moment or two later the gate creaked open.

"Come in. Hurry! *Hurry!*"

We rushed in, and he shut the gate. A jumble of cottages rose on the slope above us. The villager who'd admitted us, a man of middle age, blew twice on a horn, gaped at us, and said nothing.

Rhys performed one of his elaborate bows, and the man's jaw sank even lower.

"A sorcerer!" he said.

Meryl coughed.

He gaped at Meryl. "A maiden in a cloud!"

We didn't have time for his astonishment. "I am Princess Adelina," I said. "We need—"

"A princess!"

Villagers began to gather, and I addressed them. "We need directions to the Aisnan Valley. Who can tell us?"

No one spoke.

Meryl coughed.

"My sister is sick. Won't you help us?"

A man stepped forward. He wore a fur-trimmed cape and carried a wooden staff. "I am Dunstan, mayor here. What is this about?"

I repeated my name, and he had the grace to bow. A few others in the crowd curtsied or bowed, but not many.

"My sister is ill with the Gray Death, and she's closer to dying with every second you all waste."

A few in the crowd caught their breath.

I added, "She'll be cured if she drinks from the waterfall in the Aisnan Valley."

Everyone began talking at once.

Dunstan clapped for silence. "We've heard of this Gray Death, but none of us has ever been afflicted."

Because of the waterfall? Vollys told the truth!

The mayor continued, "If you arouse the monsters in the valley, we will suffer."

I said, "If there are monsters in our path, we'll fight them."

Meryl added, "No wonder Drualt left Bamarre after he came to Surmic village."

The mayor's face reddened. "We opened our gate to strangers. That's cour—"

Rhys raised his baton.

The mayor drew back. "Cast no spells! These are the directions: The Aisnan Valley is due north. Follow the stars and you'll find it."

"Dunstan!" A younger man threaded his way through the crowd. "They'll lose their way." He turned to us. "The path isn't marked. You have to know which turns to take. It's a long, twisting way." He stared at Meryl. "You will fight, my lady, sick as you are?"

"I will fight." She coughed.

He spoke to the crowd. "I'll lead them to the valley, and when the monsters strike, I'll fight too." He bowed to Meryl and me. "I am Gavin.

Some in Surmic have courage."

We waited while he ran to his cottage for his sword and his bow and arrows. Several others left the crowd when he did.

An old man said, "In the mountains, smart folk do not stray at night. My sister . . ." He began a tale.

How long could it take for Gavin to get his weapons?

I gave Meryl a moily herb flower to suck. Perhaps it would ease her cough.

" . . . search party went after my sister. Not one came back. My uncle . . ."

Gavin ran down the hill toward us, buckling on his sword as he came. Two men and a young woman followed him, also buckling on swords.

"We'll come too," the woman said.

Another woman and another man left the crowd to join us. They already wore their swords. The woman recited from the ending of *Drualt*.

> "Be brave, Bamarre!
> Go forth, Bamarre,
> The timid with the strong.
> Let not your heroes
> Fight alone."

Someone in the crowd began to weep. A man cried out, "Stay, Eliza!"

Dunstan told the six who had joined us, "You go at your peril."

Gavin answered, "You stay at your peril."

The gatekeeper opened the gate, and we filed out. The night was advancing. Gavin walked between me and Meryl. Rhys was on my other side. The others followed behind. Gavin set the pace, quick, but not so fast that we'd have to stop to rest.

"How long until we reach the valley?" I asked him.

"Three hours at least, if we aren't slain along the way."

Three hours! And Meryl was to die at dawn.

"You'll be a hero, Gavin," she said, "and we'll all have an adventure." Her coughing had subsided. Perhaps the moily herb had helped.

Eliza said, "There are no ogres the way we're going, but gryphons may attack. They have fine night eyes."

I looked up but saw only stars. We walked on. I asked Gavin and Eliza to describe the waterfall.

"It's very high, Your Highness," said Gavin, "and the heights from which the water descends are lost in mist."

Eliza added, "No streams flow from it. The water vanishes as soon as it touches the valley."

Again Vollys had spoken true.

She continued, "The grass under the falls, where the water lands and vanishes, is the greenest in the Eskerns. We pasture our sheep there when we are well armed. You can almost see them grow fat as they graze."

"Have you ever drunk from the falls?" Rhys asked.

Gavin answered, "When I bring the sheep, I drink the water. We all do."

They drank the water, and none of them caught the Gray Death.

Meryl began to question Gavin about his encounters with monsters. He answered, and the other villagers chimed in. Rhys touched my arm, and we fell to the back of the group.

"There is something I must say. . . ." He hesitated. "Although you may not like to hear it." He fell silent. "It concerns us. You"—he paused—"and me."

He knew I loved him. He felt he had to discourage me. "You needn't say it," I murmured.

"No, I must." His voice sounded odd, as though he had a cold, although sorcerers didn't get colds. "Orne is a fine teacher, as I've told you."

Orne had told him what to say.

"And very convincing." He stopped again, and then resumed. "But I don't always agree with him. On the subject of marriage, to humans anyway . . ."

Marriage?

". . . I think he's mistaken, especially about me. Oh, Addie, we may both die tonight. . . ."

The Eskerns must be enchanted, I thought. They were making me imagine things. But I was smiling.

He stopped and took my hand. "If we die, or if I die . . ."

He was speaking of dying, and I couldn't stop smiling.

In the dark he must not have noticed, because he said in a rush, "I must tell you that I love you, and if I live I will ask for your hand, but you needn't say anything now if it distresses you, and I might rather die without knowing that you don't love me if that's how you feel."

I tried to speak, but nothing came. I had gained courage during my adventures, but not for this.

"Addie?"

Too soft to hear, I whispered, "I do love you."

But he heard. He cupped his hand under my

chin and tilted my face up so I had to meet his eyes. He was smiling too, with a smile as happy as mine. "Oh, Addie!" He leaned down to kiss me.

But Meryl called, "Addie! Where are you? Rhys?" She sounded frightened.

"We're coming."

He picked me up and flew me to her. "We were just talking about what's to come," he said slyly.

"I thought a monster had taken you." She coughed.

I gave her another moily herb flower. We resumed walking, only now Rhys held my hand. I reached forward into the cloud blanket and caught Meryl's hand, and so I held my two loves. But Meryl's hand was as hot as a dragon.

We fell silent, all of us, and marched on. Meryl strode along and didn't seem to be tiring. I heard wings and looked up, but it was just an owl. In a moment I heard its hoot.

I wondered how far we'd gone, how far we had yet to go. I didn't ask. I didn't want the trek or the night to end. For the moment I had everything I wanted.

We walked along a ridge and then started upward, arranging ourselves in single file as the way narrowed, Meryl ahead of me, Rhys behind. I released Rhys's hand but held on to Meryl's. The path twisted and then turned back on itself and turned again. We clambered from rock to rock.

I heard wings again. Two creatures crossed the moon, gryphons or eagles. Whatever they were, they flew over and were gone.

The climb became steeper. Soon my breathing was ragged, and Meryl began to cough again, and another moily herb flower did no good.

I wasn't sure if the moon had dimmed and the sky had lightened, or if it was just my imagination. At last we reached the crest and began to walk along it. Gavin said, "The Aisnan Valley is there below us." He gestured to the left, but it was too dark to make out any details.

"We can't descend here," Eliza said. "We have to go around. Even so, it isn't far. We'll come to a ledge. A few feet beyond it is the rock we call the Sentry. When we round the Sentry, we'll be in the valley."

I asked, "How far is the waterfall from there?"

"Half a mile," said Gavin, "more or less."

Rhys could fly Meryl there. Her recovery

could be minutes away!

We walked a little distance and then began to descend. I listened for the waterfall but heard nothing. I squeezed Meryl's hand and she squeezed back, but I thought her grip had weakened.

The descent was gradual, easier than the climb.

"Nine heroes of Bamarre descended into the Aisnan Valley," Meryl said, and coughed. "We should be in a poem. Addie, would you recite something from *Drualt*?"

I began to recite from an early battle scene. At first my voice was soft, but it gained strength as I went on.

> "*King Bruce, armor shining,*
> *Led the right flank, shouting,*
> *'Hide, monsters, hide*
> *From our might.'*
> *Drualt, armor bloody,*
> *Led the left flank, shouting,*
> *'Come, monsters, come*
> *And meet our might.'*"

Everyone joined in, Rhys with his deep voice, Meryl with her hoarse one, and the villagers.

> *"King Bruce frowned,*
> *His mouth set grim, and*
> *A dread light was in*
> *His eyes. His soldiers too*
> *Were grim, and battled*
> *As a farmer plows*
> *A stony field, with a will,*
> *But no delight.*
> *Drualt laughed, and*
> *A glad light was in*
> *His eyes. His soldiers*
> *Laughed too, and fought*
> *As a lad or maid begins a dance,*
> *With a will and much delight.*
> *Bruce and his warriors*
> *Sang out—"*

I heard an echo, though there hadn't been one before.

> *"Drualt and his warriors*
> *Rang out—"*

We sounded like fifty, instead of just nine.

> *"Now carve, my sword.*
> *Now bite, my arrows.*

Now die, my enemy.
Victory for Bamarre!'"

We'd almost reached the bottom, and Gavin stopped us. "Here is the ledge. When we jump down, we'll be level with the valley."

We sat on the ledge. I thought I heard the roar of the falls. The sky was definitely beginning to brighten. Dawn would come soon. I looked at Meryl's ashy face. She was smiling. My heart began to pound.

The villagers jumped down first, about seven feet. Then I jumped, and Gavin caught me. Rhys lifted Meryl and flew her down, ignoring her protests.

Gavin pointed at a tall rock. "There's the Sentry."

I took Meryl's hand again, and we stepped into the valley.

A boulder crashed to the ground not two feet ahead of us. Rocks flew. One hit Gavin in the chest, and he fell.

Ogres were everywhere, throwing boulders and trees and huge armfuls of dirt, and thundering in their rock language.

Gavin scrambled to his feet. A tree trunk thudded into the rock above us. It caromed off and landed. Eliza's foot was caught under the roots.

I helped the villagers free her foot. Screeches and yawps filled the air. Gryphons, a hundred or more, swooped down on us.

Meryl shouted, her voice breaking, "Victory for Bamarre!"

Chapter Twenty-eight

Meryl began to run toward the falls. Rhys picked her up and started flying with her while three gryphons attacked him. I groped in my bundle for the magic tablecloth. Meryl shouted, "Put me down! Let me fight."

"Take her to the waterfall!" I shouted.

But he had to set her down so he could defend them both. I saw her don the magic cloak and become just a shimmer and a glimmer in the gloom before the dawn.

I ran to them while still fumbling for the tablecloth. I had almost reached them when a rock hit my shoulder. I staggered and fell. An ogre loomed over me, his face cracked in laughter.

I scrambled away. He reached for me. Missed by inches. I drew my sword. He grabbed up a boulder. I stumbled back. He raised the boulder.

He shrieked and dropped the boulder. Blood poured from his knee. I heard Meryl's voice, "There, ogre. Run, Addie."

I ran—to her, to the shadow she was in the

cloak. The ogre raised the boulder again.

He fell, his throat cut, and I saw Rhys fly off, fighting a gryphon.

"Get Meryl," I shouted, but he didn't hear.

A gryphon landed on me, knocking me over. I stabbed up at it. My sword bit flesh, and then—the gryphon disappeared. I heard faint laughter.

"A specter!" Meryl breathed next to my ear. She shouted to everyone, "Some gryphons are specters." Then, softly again, "Take care. I'm off to the waterfall."

A shadow shifted, and she was gone. Another gryphon on me! I stabbed its belly, and it fell away, bleeding. With my other hand I kept trying to find the tablecloth.

A gryphon knocked me down. I stabbed wildly, cut a claw. The gryphon bit my cheek and pinned my sword arm with a wing. It bit again. It was eating me!

Beady, bloodshot eye. I poked it—pressed hard—felt wetness. Its head shot back. Squawks. I grabbed its neck. Squeezed. It tried to fly, dragged me instead and released my arm. I squeezed with both hands. Its wings beat at me. I hung on. Squeezed. A boulder crashed, near, so near. Still I held. Squeezed. Squeezed.

The gryphon shrieked.

I squeezed.

I heard choking. Its head drooped. I let go. It fell away.

"Meryl, I strangled a gryphon!" I yelled, although I hoped she was too far away to hear.

I reached into my bundle. At last—the table-cloth.

Another gryphon dived at me. I whipped out the cloth. "Good-table-set-thy-cloth."

Nothing happened.

The gryphon was on me, claws in my shoulder. Words tumbled out: "Good-tablecloth-please-set-thyself." The cloth unfolded. The gryphon stopped, its beak an inch from my bloody cheek. A roast popped out. The gryphon leaped on the food. More dishes. Another gryphon landed on the tablecloth. The swarm descended.

Where was Meryl? Had she reached the falls? Any minute the sun would rise.

I began to run. A tree trunk whizzed by my ear. Eliza loosed an arrow. An ogre dropped a boulder, slowed, fell.

Where was Meryl?

There was Gavin, halfway to the falls, fighting a gryphon. An ogre lumbered at him.

I shouted. "Gavin!"

The ogre bellowed and clawed at his own

back. He turned, and I saw Meryl riding him, the cloak no longer much protection. Her sword flashed. Blood spurted from the ogre's neck. He pitched over. She stood and ran toward the falls.

I raced to catch up. An ogre leaped between us, his head and shoulders swathed in cloud. Another cloud-ogre lurched about nearby.

Rhys hovered, just higher than the ogres' heads, pointing his baton at one ogre, then another, wrapping them in clouds.

I ran by. An ogre came at Meryl. She stabbed him in the belly. She was laughing.

A boulder landed. Rocks flew, hit my forehead, my shoulder, my aching ribs. I reeled, couldn't breathe.

Meryl ran to me, supported me. "Addie—"

I gasped for air. "To the falls!" I grabbed her hand.

We ran.

Rhys flew at my right, protecting us with baton and sword.

Blood in my eye. I blinked it away.

Wait, sun! Wait, dawn!

Eliza and Gavin ran at my left, thrusting, stabbing.

A gryphon swooped down on us. I stabbed. Meryl stabbed. It vanished.

I heard the waterfall.

We ran.

Meryl was laughing. "Die, monsters! Victory for Bamarre!"

I shouted too. "Victory for Meryl!"

Wait, sun! Wait, dawn! Victory for Meryl!

An ogre blocked us. Eliza and Gavin rushed at him.

Eliza fell. Gavin shrieked.

Meryl and I ran around tree trunks, boulders, rocks. Rhys killed another gryphon.

We ran. I saw the waterfall, still a quarter mile off.

A shadow fell over us. I smelled metal and heard bells.

Vollys.

She landed before us, blocking our way.

She surveyed the fighting. "I prepared this welcome for you, little princess." The grass between her belly and front leg was staining red. She still bled from the wound I'd given her.

Meryl murmured, "A dragon! It's beautiful."

"Ah. This is the sister. Brave as my Willard. So sad that the sun will rise in seven minutes." Her tail whipped around and snatched up Meryl and me. "Home we go." She spread her wings. "Little one, as we fly, tell your sister farewell. I—"

Rhys soared by, pointing his baton. Her head became wrapped in cloud.

The cloud turned orange as she flamed.

An ogre threw a boulder at us and hit her tail.

It lifted. My head snapped back. The tail felled the ogre. My head snapped forward. The tail slammed us into the ground. Pain shot up my legs. But the tail loosened its grip.

Meryl and I wriggled free. The scales scraped—little knives.

"Run, Meryl!"

I saw Vollys's claw, curled, underside up. I raised my sword, but Meryl stabbed first.

Vollys yelped.

I started toward Meryl.

Rhys sent more cloud.

Vollys flamed at him, trumpeting, "All die before me!"

Rhys stabbed her in the eye. She flamed again. His cloak caught! He fell from the sky!

I swerved, shouting to Meryl, "To the falls!" Meryl ran.

Vollys reared up, her eye streaming. I saw a black nostril. A fiery mouth opened.

"Run, Meryl!" I hurled my sword with all my strength—more than all my strength. Hurled my sword—into Vollys's throat.

She choked. No flame. She swayed. She was bleeding, bleeding.

Meryl raced toward the waterfall. *Sun, don't rise!*

Vollys toppled.

Her neck landed on my arm. I was trapped, staring into her huge face.

She gasped, "Mourn for me, little princess."

I struggled to free my arm.

"I would have mourned for you."

I puffed, "Move your neck and I will mourn."

A small bell. "Ah, little princess, you amuse me still." She tried. A vein stood out in her neck. She shifted, a little. Enough.

Meryl! I saw a sword on the grass. Rhys's sword. I took it.

Vollys wheezed, "Mourn for . . ."

I heard her death rattle. *Sun, don't rise!* I ran around her corpse.

There was Meryl, trying to run while stabbing a gryphon. I sprinted toward her and saw the gryphon fall away. Its wing beat the ground once and was still. Meryl ran.

I ran too, fighting for breath. The falls roared in my ears. Meryl had only a few more yards to go.

A tree trunk sailed over her head.

Sun, don't rise!

Huge hands circled my ribs. An ogre raised me to his chest. I heard his rock laugh. He squeezed. Pain made me scream.

Till my dying day I will wish I hadn't screamed. Meryl heard me. She turned. She started running back for me.

"No! Go on!" I stabbed at the ogre's arms. He grunted but still held me.

The sun rose over an eastern peak. Meryl staggered.

Golden rays spread across the valley. Meryl dropped, facedown.

I stabbed upward. The ogre shrieked and released me. I threw myself down at Meryl's side, gently rolled her over.

Her eyelids fluttered. "Addie?"

I could barely hear her.

"This was our finest day." She sighed, and her eyes closed.

"Meryl! Don't die!"

I stood up, wailing—

And a boulder smashed into my chest.

I collapsed.

I felt raindrops.

Then nothing.

Chapter Twenty-nine

I smelled peonies. Someone was singing.
Meryl. Rhys. I began to cry with my eyes
squeezed shut.

"Princess Addie? Are you awake?" I didn't
recognize the man's voice, although it sounded
familiar. He continued. "Don't cry. Laugh.
Laugh!"

"You can open your eyes. There's nothing to
fear." I knew that voice—Meryl!

I opened my eyes. There she was, smiling at
me. Cured. Well again.

A huge young man stood next to her, grinning down at me. Who was he?

And where was I? I was in a bed, but not in
Bamarre castle.

It didn't matter. Meryl was well. I cried
harder than before. I was happy, but I couldn't
stop crying.

"She's still weak. Here, give her this."

I turned my head and saw Milton. I choked
out, "How did you get here?"

He passed a steaming mug to Meryl. "Your sister sent for me."

Meryl sat next to me and put her free hand behind my shoulders to prop me up. I leaned against her and took the mug. I smelled the moily herb. Milton piled pillows behind me. I sipped the tea, still crying. That was all I could do—sip, stare at Meryl, weep.

I leaned back into the pillows so I could see her better. I saw no hint she'd ever been sick. I would have expected the Gray Death to have marked her, but it hadn't. Her eyes were clear, and the ashy gray was gone from her face.

Something had changed, though. I thought she looked older. Then I wasn't sure. Maybe she looked younger.

It made no difference. She was healthy. I wished I could stop crying about it.

"Drink your tea while it's hot."

Bella's voice. She was here too, standing to the right of the huge stranger. Her eyes were red. She'd also been crying.

I didn't see Rhys. I wanted to see him. More tears splashed into my tea. Meryl placed a cool hand on my forehead. The last time I'd felt that hand, it had been burning up with fever.

As soon as she touched me, I felt calmer and my tears stopped flowing.

I found my voice again. "Rhys?"

"He's resting," Meryl said.

"He was afire," I said. "He—"

The stranger said, "He'll be fine, Princess Addie." He laughed. "He'll be ready for more dragons soon."

I wondered again who the man was. He looked like someone I knew, yet I'd never met him before. He was taller than the tallest of Father's guards, and he had curly black hair and a curly black beard.

He repeated, "He'll be fine, Princess Addie."

That made me remember the others. "The villagers, are they fine too?"

"Gavin died," Meryl said. "An ogre killed him. The rest are well."

I swallowed. "The first one to help us."

The stranger spoke again. "Because of him Surmic is no longer a place of shame."

I supposed, but . . . "Living heroes are better," I said.

"We have you for that," Bella said, her voice cracking at the end.

I blushed. "And Meryl too."

"I'm not a hero as you are."

I thought she looked unhappy for a

moment, and I wondered if she envied me for finding the cure.

She smiled and looked happy again. "I'm so proud of you, Addie."

I blushed again and couldn't meet her eyes. I covered my embarrassment by looking around the room.

I supposed I was in a bedchamber, since I was in a bed. But this room was built on a larger scale than any in Bamarre castle. The distant walls were white marble, hung with enormous tapestries depicting Drualt's adventures. The floors were coral-colored marble. I couldn't see the ceiling, which was hidden by the canopy on my four-poster bed, but the canopy itself was high enough to be an ordinary ceiling.

One thing was odd—I didn't see a fireplace.

"It's pretty here," I said, and swallowed the last of my tea.

A sob broke from Bella.

"What's wrong?" I said.

"You're too weak for . . ." She stopped. "You're too weak."

She frightened me. I turned to Milton. "Am I dying, and is everyone afraid to tell me?"

"You're not dying," he said. "You need more rest, that's all."

I decided not to worry about Bella, then. I already felt better. The moily herb had worked its usual magic. I sat up and asked Meryl, "How long did it take for the waterfall to cure you?"

"It didn't. It *was* the cure, but it didn't cure me."

I felt confused.

She went on. "Vollys told you the truth. Remember the prophecy?"

"The Gray Death will be cured when cowards find courage and rain falls over all Bamarre."

"Your courage made the cure possible, and the rain was the cure itself. While they rescued you and the others, the fairies sent the same waterfall water down in a rainstorm over all Bamarre. The Gray Death is gone forever."

I leaned forward. "Fairies rescued us? Real fairies?"

The stranger laughed. "Real fairies, Princess Addie."

Meryl began, "They—"

"Did you meet any of them? Couldn't you have awakened me?" I looked reproachfully from Meryl to Bella.

But the stranger answered again. "You needed to sleep. It would have been cruel to wake you." He laughed. "But there's a chance you might still meet a fairy or two. You might already—"

Now? It dawned on me. "Are we . . . Could this . . . Are we in their castle?"

Meryl nodded, smiling.

I wondered why she wasn't more excited.

"You've changed," I told her. "The Gray Death left its mark on you."

"No-o-o," Meryl said slowly. "The Gray Death didn't change me."

"Then what did? You're different now. And what did you mean about the cure not curing you?" I was becoming uneasy. It wasn't only her not being excited about fairies. There was more—calming me just by touching my forehead, and looking older and younger at the same time.

No one answered me. Meryl's smile turned uncertain. Bella wept, and even Milton looked sad.

"When you're better, Addie, she'll tell you," Bella said. "Until then—"

"I'm well enough. Tell me now. Meryl, didn't the fairies rescue you too?"

"In a way." She tucked my hair behind my ears, and her touch soothed me again. "The rain cured everyone who had the Gray Death—except one or two who were moments from death, as I was." Her voice was more even than it used to be.

"What happened to them?" I was almost shouting. "What happened to you?"

Bella broke in. "She's too weak, Meryl . . . I mean, My Lady. Wait until—"

Why did Bella call her "My Lady"? I leaned forward. "Tell me!"

"The others died, Addie." Meryl looked utterly serene, calmer than I'd ever seen her. Calmer than she'd looked in life, when she was always striving for something.

In life! What was I thinking? She was alive now, talking to me.

I didn't want to ask the next question, but I did. "How were you cured if none of the others were?"

"I'm hungry," the stranger said, "and I'll warrant that a feast awaits us." He smiled down at me. "You're a rare brave maid." He patted my foot through the covers, and his touch soothed just as Meryl's had. Then he left the room, stepping gracefully for such a giant.

Milton straightened my bedclothes and then followed the stranger out.

Bella stood over me. "Addie . . ." She shook her head, and a tear landed on my hand. She turned to Meryl. "Remember—she's not as strong as you were." She left.

"You are strong," Meryl said after Bella had closed the door behind her. "You're stronger than I was, stronger than I had any idea of."

"I had no idea either. You could have started your adventures years ago and taken me along." Now that she was ready to answer my questions, I was reluctant to hear. "I'll come in the future, though." I would too. I had made a promise in Vollys's cave, and I would keep it. I would help Meryl save Bamarre. Rhys would help too.

She shook her head.

"Yes, I will," I said. "I want to be near you from today on."

"I will always be nearby."

"Good. That's settled. However, I'm tired again. I think I'll go back to sleep." I wriggled down into the bed and closed my eyes.

"Addie?" Her tone changed. "Listen. . . . Please open your eyes."

Now she sounded exactly like her old self.

"Meryl?"

She looked just as she used to when she was planning something forbidden—excited and happy and bursting with energy. She picked up my left hand and ran her fingers lightly across my knuckles. "Suppose I had a chance at adventures that were greater even than fighting monsters, greater than anything Bamarre can offer. Suppose I couldn't be slain or even hurt in these adventures. I might not win—I might even lose—"

"It would be an odd adventure if you couldn't get hurt." I thought about it. "Nice, but it wouldn't be a real adventure."

She frowned in mock annoyance. "You're not letting me finish. Suppose the adventures *are* real. Suppose the stakes are enormously high, even if I'm in no danger. Suppose I want to go on these adventures more than I ever wanted to do anything. Suppose I'm *abjectly* grateful at the chance to go on these adventures. But suppose you couldn't come with me, suppose I couldn't even tell you much about them. Would you—"

"But I have to come. I told you, I want you nearby." I laughed, holding her hand tightly. "I'd especially want to go if we couldn't get hurt." I added impulsively, "Oh, it's so wonderful to have you back, your old self back." I squeezed her hand.

"I'm doing this all wrong." Meryl's voice had changed again, to something between my familiar Meryl and the new calm Meryl. "I'm not my old self anymore. That is, part of me is, but most of me isn't. The fairies couldn't cure me, Addie. I was too near death. So they offered me a way to live, a different way. It was a great honor.

"They offered to transform me into a fairy, and I said yes."

Chapter Thirty

Impossible! She couldn't be a fairy. She was sitting here next to me, breathing in and out just as I was, as human as I was.

Yes, she was different—she'd gone insane. That was the difference. The Gray Death had robbed her of her mind.

"I know it's hard to believe, Addie. I'd never . . ."

Why did Bella and Milton leave me alone to find out she was crazy?

". . . not the first person to become a fairy. We remember what it was to be human—the other fairies don't know. And Addie, the love stays."

I couldn't think what to say. "It must be pleasant to be a fairy," I said, trying to speak as usual. "I'd like to try it myself."

She laughed. "Addie, Addie. I'm telling the truth. I'm a fairy now."

Maybe she was teasing me. But the joke wasn't funny, and she had never been cruel.

She stood up. "How can I prove it to you?"

"You can't."

She paced in a small circle. After a minute or two, she said, "Perhaps this will convince you." She took my empty mug from the table next to the bed and upended it over her hand. A few drops spilled out. One of them kept its shape in her hand and began to swell.

She resumed her seat next to me. "Watch."

The drop grew to be a huge wet bubble the size of a cabbage. A scene took shape inside. I saw myself in there. I was crossing the drawbridge at Bamarre castle, wearing a serving maid's gown and carrying a sack.

That scene dissolved, and another took its place. I saw myself in the magic boots. I was skimming along the ground and pulling an ogre after me.

In the next scene I saw myself, stepping warily through Mulee Forest. More scenes of my quest followed. I couldn't look away, although I kept thinking, I'm dreaming. This is delirium.

Finally the scene in the Aisnan Valley appeared. It was the end of the battle, or the end of my part in it. I saw myself climb out of the grip of Vollys's tail, saw Meryl stab Vollys's claw. Then Vollys flamed at Rhys; he fell; I heaved my sword into Vollys's throat; she freed my arm; the boulder smashed into my chest.

The scene went on, showing me what had followed, the part I hadn't seen. The sky darkened. Lightning flashed, and rain fell, putting out the dragon fires that still raged.

"Now watch," Meryl said—as though I'd look away!

The valley was lit again, not by the sun, but by whorls of colored light that drifted down from a mountain I had somehow not seen before. Within each bright whorl I made out a figure, not human but human shaped.

These beings of light bent over us, picked us up, and floated upward with us. I kept my eyes on the beings that carried Meryl and Rhys and me. But the scene shifted. I saw a being place me on a bed—this bed. Then the being bent over me. Its light engulfed me for a moment, no more. The being straightened and floated from the chamber, leaving me alone.

The scene shifted again, and I saw Rhys treated just as I had been. Another shift, and I saw Meryl on a bed, surrounded by many of the beings of light, a throng of them.

I saw Meryl sit up. Meryl, my Meryl!

"They could make me well for a little while, long enough for me to decide."

In the bubble, Meryl's face was rapt. She

was listening to something. A moment later she laughed, while tears rolled down her cheeks.

"That's when they offered me the choice of death or transformation. Before, I would have thought it would be easy to decide, but it wasn't. The choice would last forever. Forever. Eternity—no going back, no changing my mind.

"But in one way there was no choice. Either way I'd lose you. Either way I'd stop being a human sister and stop having a human sister."

In the bubble Meryl said something.

"That's when I chose to be a fairy."

I saw her lie back on the bed, and all the beings engulfed her. After a few seconds, they backed away from the bed. A new being, a new whorl, rose up. I gasped. "No!"

Then it was over. The bubble shrank and became a droplet again. The being next to me, the one who looked like Meryl, dried her hand on her gown.

I rolled over and wept into my pillows.

A hand stroked my hair, patted my back. I felt the comfort but went on crying. I hadn't saved Meryl. My quest had failed. The Gray Death had killed her after all. If I hadn't screamed when the ogre had grabbed me, she would have reached the waterfall in time. If I hadn't waited so long to take up the quest, she would have lived. If I'd reached the Aisnan Valley before she'd been so near the end, dawn wouldn't have mattered, and the water would have cured her. Now I'd lost her, and it was my fault.

The fairy stroked my back, and I cried on and on. I'd miss loving my sister. Loving her had changed me, had made me brave. Loving her was the best part of me.

I don't know how long I cried. Finally, I rolled over and peered up at the fairy through eyes that stung from so much weeping.

"Why do you look the same as you used to?" Almost the same.

"I'm accustomed to this shape. Several other fairies used to be human. They prefer to be this way, and so do I."

"Do you miss your old self?"

"She's still in me."

But the human Meryl was frozen in the past, locked inside the fairy. The human Meryl would no longer feel things on her own, would no longer grow and change.

More tears came. "It's all my fault."

"It's *not* your fault. You saved me. If not for you, I'd be dead."

"If I had left home earlier, you'd be alive, and you'd be human."

"Perhaps. But still, none of it was your fault. The Gray Death chose me. It might have chosen you, but it chose me." She stroked my wet cheeks. "I used to wonder if I was secretly glad that I'd promised not to begin my adventures until you were married. I thought I might have promised because I was really a coward."

That was absurd. She was never a coward. And it was my fault. She just didn't realize. "If I hadn't screamed when that ogre snatched me, you would have contin—"

She put her fingers over my lips. "No, Addie, that was my fault. I should have gone on to the falls. I should have known you could overcome an ogre. I had seen how much you'd changed."

"But . . ." She was right. I had changed, and I did overcome the ogre. "But it wasn't your fault for wanting to rescue me."

"I'm not sure, but it makes no difference. It was all part of that glorious day. I'm so grateful to you for bringing me to the battle in the Aisnan Valley, because I discovered there that I was brave. You brought me to an adventure and gave me the chance to be a hero, which is all I ever wanted."

"It's not all I wanted," I said. But her words comforted me somewhat, and they brought an understanding that had eluded me before. I finally saw the real difference between Meryl and me, truer than the difference between cowardly and brave. She wanted to battle monsters for the adventure of it. I wanted to defeat them for the peace that would follow.

"I missed you," the fairy Meryl said. "I missed you while you were gone. I was proud of you for going, but I was afraid that you wouldn't get back in time to tell me good-bye. I was afraid even while the Gray Death made me sleep. I've missed you here too, while you were healing. I'm so glad you're awake now. I'm so glad I've regained you."

"It's not the same, though." I thought about returning to Bamarre castle without her. Father had one daughter now. His firstborn was gone.

The fairy Meryl looked sad too. "You're right. It's not the same, and it won't be the same. Fairies don't have sisters."

Her sadness was the best comfort, oddly enough. She missed being a sister too. It made me hug her, and when I did, when she hugged me tight, I found oceans of comfort, galaxies of comfort.

Chapter Thirty-one

After a time Meryl left me, and I fell asleep again.

I'm not sure how long I slept. I awoke several times, and she was always there. Sometimes I wept again, grief mixed with joy. Sometimes I only filled my eyes with her.

At last I awoke and knew my convalescence was over. This time I was alone. I sat up and swung my legs over the edge of the bed. A gown was draped across two chairs.

It was a fairy gown, deep purple, with a gathered skirt that revealed a pale-violet underskirt. I touched the skirt, half expecting it to give off sparks. It didn't, and the cloth was oh so soft, as soft as the cloth Rhys had given me an age ago.

Rhys!

I had asked Meryl for news of him whenever I awoke, but her report was always that he was resting. Now I would see for myself.

I dressed quickly. Not surprisingly, the gown fit me perfectly.

Someone knocked on my door. I opened it, and Meryl came in.

Standing up, dressed, no longer a weepy invalid, I felt shy with her. It came to me in a new way that she was a *fairy*.

"You've changed too, you know," she said, understanding my look, or reading my mind—I was afraid to think which. "You're not the timid little sister anymore. I'd feel shy meeting the new Addie—that is, if I were ever shy to begin with." She grinned.

I felt easier. I asked about Rhys, and she said he was still resting. I couldn't even look in on him, she said. Since sorcerers don't sleep, he needed dark and quiet to get better. She said Milton was sitting outside his chamber. He had sworn to fetch me the moment Rhys was well enough for a visit.

I asked her to take me to Milton, because I had a few questions. She did, and we found the elf knitting as always, seated on a three-legged stool, looking smaller than usual next to the huge carved door to Rhys's chamber. He jumped up when he saw us and put his knitting down on the stool.

"Addie! You're well again." He hurried toward us and looked me up and down. "Completely well."

"How is Rhys?"

"He's mending."

"Why is it taking so long?"

Milton shrugged. "It takes as long as it takes. In the end he'll be as well as you are."

"Are you certain?" I wished the door were thinner and I could hear something, Rhys breathing or rolling over.

"Does he speak?" I asked next. Does he speak of me?

"When I go in to make sure he's comfortable, he always asks after you."

Always! Every time! I grinned foolishly.

"Tell him . . . tell him I've been to see you. Tell him I said he should mend as hard as he can and as fast as he can. Tell him . . ." I stopped. Tell him what?

Tell him I love him.

He knew that. "Tell him I miss him."

Meryl and I left. She gave me a tour of the fairy castle and its gardens. The castle was vast, and the corridors seemed to twist and turn endlessly. I hoped I would never have to find my chamber on my own. The walls of the corridors and the chambers were hung with enormous tapestries depicting Drualt's adventures. I examined one closely, comparing it to my own efforts in watercolor and embroidery. The colors were richer than any I ever had, and the realism was astonishing.

Meryl said, "Your portrayals have more feeling, Addie."

I was glad to hear it, but I thought she was wrong. "What adventure is this?" It wasn't in *Drualt*. "What monster is that?"

It resembled a huge winged crab that breathed fire like a dragon and had knife-sharp pincers.

"That's Idrid. It's the only one of its kind. Drualt fought it for a week before he finally defeated it."

I was about to ask her how she knew about an adventure that wasn't in *Drualt*, but then I remembered. She was a fairy. She'd know.

We left the castle, and Meryl showed me the gardens, where spring flowers and the flowers of summer and fall bloomed together. I heard again the singing that I'd first awakened to.

It was the pink sunrise or sunset of a fine warm day. As we wandered, I noticed that the sun never rose nor set. It only trembled on the brink, eternally full of promise.

"How high up are we?" I asked. "How tall is Mount Ziriat?"

"It's half again as tall as the tallest peak in the Eskerns."

"Are any creatures in Bamarre able to see it?"

"Not one. Not even dragons, although they know where it is."

I wondered how it could be so warm here when we were so high up. A fairy came toward us on the path. It was one of the whorl-of-light fairies. I curtsied and didn't dare look up until it had passed. But then I stared hard at the retreating figure. It seemed to glide more than walk, reminding me of a breeze made visible.

"Meryl, how does it feel to be a fairy?"

"I don't know if I can describe it." She was silent. "Humans . . . No, that's not right. I used to have keen eyesight. Do you remember?"

Of course I did.

"It's even better now." She took a deep breath. "I can see farther than you can with your spyglass, and I can look at you at the same time. From right here I feel the heat in the Bamarrian desert. I feel a teaspoon of sand slide off a sand dune. I hear the wind whistle around the stars. If I need to, I can leave you for a moment to move a star."

To move a star? Why would she need to do that?

"You said being a fairy meant having more important adventures than you could have in Bamarre. What sort of adventures?"

She took my hand and led me to a bench. "Come. Milton says you shouldn't overdo."

We sat down.

"Bamarre and the other kingdoms float on a vast ocean, right?"

I nodded. Every child knew that. The kingdoms floated on a vast ocean under a vast sky.

"Under a vast sky. There are monsters deep in the ocean and high in the sky who threaten all the kingdoms. They're wondrous, Addie! Wondrous and terrible!"

She sounded exactly as she used to.

"Idrid is one of them, and not the worst one. Some are . . ."

If Idrid was a monster in the world beyond Bamarre, then how could Drualt have fought it?

". . . than ogres, and some are cleverer and wilier than dragons, and one I know of is hungrier and greedier than all the gryphons combined."

Were they real? I wondered, looking up. It seemed that I could see forever through the clear sky, and I saw no monsters.

Meryl looked up too. "Eternal night hovers above our daylight. We fight monsters in that inky dark. We can see through it, and so can they. A host of fairies is fighting now. I'm to join them." She stopped, and her unspoken words hung in the air. She would join them, and I would return to Bamarre without her.

I swallowed over the lump in my throat and tried to keep the misery out of my voice. "Will you really be safe? Are you sure you can't be hurt?"

She took my hand. "I'm sure. They can't hurt me. None of them can."

"If they can't hurt you, don't you always defeat them?"

"No. They're not trying to kill us, they're trying to destroy Bamarre and the other kingdoms. Sometimes they carry the day, and you humans suffer, or the elves or sorcerers or dwarfs suffer. For example, Bamarre's monsters are the results of a lost battle. Raging storms are battles that . . ."

She stopped, and seemed to be listening. "In a few minutes another fairy will join us." She smiled, and for a moment I thought she was blushing. "He was with us the first time you woke up."

"The tall stranger?"

She nodded.

"What's his name?"

"Drualt."

Chapter Thirty-two

"**D**rualt?"

She just grinned at me.

"*Drualt?*"

Now she was laughing. "I should have introduced you before, but I worried—"

"*The* Drualt?"

"*The* Drualt. You should see your face, Addie. Drualt's the one—"

"How did he get here? Didn't he die hundreds—"

"The fairies rescued him too. He's a fairy now."

"Drualt? A fairy? Really?"

She laughed at me.

I pulled my hand away from hers. "Meryl, don't tease."

"I'm not. If not—"

"But he looks so young."

"He was only nineteen when Freya died. Remember? Anyway, fairies don't get wrinkles."

"Oh." This gladdened me. Meryl would be young forever. For eternity.

She must have known what I was thinking again, because she put her arm around my shoulder and squeezed. Then she released me, and her voice was brisk. "If it hadn't been for Drualt, the monsters would have slain every one of us in the Aisnan Valley."

"He was there? I didn't see him."

"He was there."

I couldn't take it in. He was there. Drualt was there. Finally I said, "Did he slay all the monsters?"

"No, but he brought the other fairies down to us, and he helped carry us here."

"Why did he save us?"

"He'll tell you. In truth, he was with you for some of your earlier adventures too."

He was with me? Then I understood. He was the one who'd helped me. The merry presence, the hand on my shoulder, my invisible ally. Drualt.

"I'll introduce you to each other."

Meet Drualt? Introduce me? As though he were an ordinary person . . . or even an ordinary fairy. Meet Drualt!

How would I talk to him?

We waited on the bench. While Meryl hummed a tune I didn't recognize, my hands turned icy cold.

After a few minutes the stranger—Drualt!—turned out of a covered path hung over with roses. A few leaves and several yellow rose petals clung to his hair.

"You're well again!" he boomed at me.

I stood and curtsied. I could barely look at him.

Meryl jumped up and laughed. "You're too tall for the rose walk, Dru. Bend over."

He did, and she dusted off his hair. Then he straightened.

"Drualt, may I introduce the Princess Adelina. Addie, may I present Drualt."

I had never felt shyer. I curtsied again.

"No need for that. I gave up bowing long ago." He laughed. "*Very* long ago."

I gulped. My heart was pounding wildly. "Thank you for helping me." I'd spoken to Drualt! I took a deep breath and hoped I wouldn't faint. "You saved my life many—"

"Oh, I don't know. You're a doughty warrior, Princess Addie, as my Freya was. As . . ." He took Meryl's hand. "As my dear Meryl is."

I blinked in astonishment.

They went on smiling at each other for a moment or two, and then Drualt said, "You must be hungry. Getting well is hard work."

Meryl was apologetic. "I should have thought. Come, Addie. There's always food here."

I followed them back to the castle, marveling at the sight of them and pinching myself.

Except for frequent trips to Milton for news of Rhys, I spent the next two days with Meryl and Drualt. I conquered my shyness with him a thousand times more quickly than I'd have dreamed possible. He was so much at ease and so jolly that I couldn't stay uncomfortable.

I begged him and Meryl for advice on how to defeat the monsters of Bamarre. I was determined to confront Father when I got home and to begin an assault against them as soon as possible.

Then I remembered. Father was going to follow Meryl and me with an army!

"Did Father ever reach the Aisnan Valley?"

Meryl laughed. "He's still asking *Homely Truths* whether he should go or not."

I laughed too. It didn't matter.

Drualt and Meryl were full of ideas for monster strategy. In our first day of conferring we talked mainly about ogres and gryphons and specters. Meryl loved my tale about the gryphons and the magic tablecloth. She thought we might be able to rid ourselves of all the creatures at once if we prepared a big enough feast.

Drualt suggested that we try to make a treaty with the ogres. "Catch one and make him talk to you," he said. "They speak the human languages if they have to. Let the captive be your ambassador. They may see reason if they know you're resolute and you won't turn tail."

Specters would be more difficult, Drualt thought. He didn't believe we'd ever be completely rid of them. He advised us to build towns and villages close to Mulee Forest. "Crowd the monsters out. Build roads through the forest. Be vigilant, and no one should go about alone. It's much harder for them to fool two at once."

We spent most of the second day talking about dragons, and we weren't through when we sat down to dinner in the fairies' cavernous dining hall. I was feeling sad about Vollys, mourning her after all, because she'd been clever and fascinating. I remembered the fun she'd had over *Homely Truths* and her love for King Willard. If only she hadn't been a dragon.

"Do you have to slay all the dragons?" Meryl said. "They're so beautiful."

They were, and Bamarre could learn much from them.

Bella snorted. "Filthy, murdering—"

"Perhaps if we saved them from their loneliness, they—"

I noticed movement and a flash of color at the doorway to the dining hall.

"*Rhys!*" I pushed back my chair and began to run to him.

He flew to me and lifted me into the air. "I didn't trust Milton when he said you were well. I had to see for myself." He smoothed the hair away from my forehead. "You are well, aren't you?"

I nodded. There was a puckered scar above his left eyebrow. I touched it. "Does it hurt?"

"No." He tightened his hold on me. "The fairies let me keep it. It makes me look dashing."

He looked wonderful—dashing or not—and he sounded just like himself.

With his free hand, he pulled the golden baton out of his sleeve and pointed it at the open window.

Nothing happened.

I laughed at his surprised face. "There are no clouds here," I said.

"I wanted to wrap us in one and kiss you. I

suppose I'll have to . . ." He raised me in his arms and kissed my left eyelid. Then his lips found my mouth.

I tasted delight—and heard the satisfied sighs of the fairies below. I didn't care. We kissed again.

Chapter Thirty-three

The next morning Meryl helped me select a wedding gown from a bewildering array of possibilities.

The gown we finally settled on was hyacinth-blue silk with a generous train. The skirt, which was scattered with diamonds, rustled delicately when I took a step and draped itself becomingly when I stopped. The bodice was cut low to reveal pale-yellow lace at my neck, and the sleeves were slashed to let more lace peep through. Meryl caught my hair up in a silk net, over which she placed a silver tiara edged with pearls. Last of all, she fastened around my neck the silver chain on which hung the empty marriage charm, a tiny jeweled box, which would be filled during the ceremony. Then she led me to a mirror.

I hardly knew myself. The maiden in the mirror was lovely—but more than lovely, she was *assured*. Not timid, not afraid of her own voice or of shadows lurking in corners. The maiden in the mirror looked resolute, strong-willed. The maiden in the mirror could lead a kingdom.

The figure next to me in the mirror was smiling and had tears in her eyes at the same time. I turned and hugged her, and we both wept a little.

"We should hurry," Meryl said finally. "Rhys will worry that you've reconsidered." She passed her hand across my eyes. They stopped smarting, and I saw in the mirror that the signs of my tears were gone.

We proceeded together to the fairies' great hall, where Drualt would perform the ceremony. Rhys was already there, lighting up the hall with his wedding costume—a slashed scarlet doublet with a chartreuse shirt poking through, hose striped in chartreuse and black, and a red plumed cap. With Rhys was his teacher, Orne, garbed in sober brown and looking displeased. The fairies had brought him here for the occasion.

Bella, Meryl, and Milton stood with me. Orne and the Surmic villagers stood with Rhys. Father was going to come, but he decided not to after reading in *Homely Truths*, "A queen bee is no gadfly, and a ship in harbor is not at sea."

Drualt cleared his throat and began the traditional stanzas from *Drualt*. They hadn't been said at weddings in his day, naturally, but they'd been said in Bamarre for centuries now.

> *"Drualt took Freya's warm hand,*
> *Her strong hand,*
> *Her sword hand,*
> *And pressed it to his lips,*
> *Pressed it . . ."*

Drualt's voice wavered. He pulled a handkerchief from the pouch at his waist and blew his nose. Then he began again.

> *"Drualt took Freya's warm hand,*
> *Her strong hand . . ."*

He faltered again. Meryl left me and stood next to him. She began to recite, and he joined in.

> *"Drualt took Freya's warm hand,*
> *Her strong hand,*
> *Her sword hand,*
> *And pressed it to his lips,*
> *Pressed it to his heart.*
> *'Come with me,' he said.*
> *'Come with me to battle,*
> *My love. Tarry at my side.*

> *Stay with me*
> *When battle is done.*
> *Tarry at my side.*
> *Laugh with me,*
> *And walk with me*
> *The long, long way.*
> *Tarry with me,*
> *My love, at my side.'"*

Every one of us in the wedding party was weeping, except Orne. But then we laughed at the ridiculousness of it, and that was better, and we were able to proceed. Drualt told us to swear the five Bamarrian marriage oaths. Rhys and I spoke in unison, and I felt in my chest the reverberations of his deeper voice. We promised to be kind to each other, to be patient, to forgive each other's faults, to be steadfast and true, and to keep joy in our love.

Then Bella produced the golden scissors from her reticule. I clipped two strands of Rhys's silky black hair, and he clipped two strands of my brown locks. We twisted the strands together, while Meryl sang,

> *"Twist and twine*
> *Your days with mine,*
> *Your years with mine.*

Cling close and never part.
Twist and twine
Your hairs with mine."

I pushed my twist of hair into the marriage charm that Meryl had placed around my neck. Rhys did the same with his twist and his charm.

We were wed. He was Prince Rhys, and I was a sorcerer's wife.

Three days later Rhys and I and Bella and Milton and the villagers left Mount Ziriat. The fairies provided us with horses, ordinary mortal horses. Meryl accompanied us down the mountain to the Aisnan Valley. At the falls she stopped. Rhys drew everyone aside so she and I could be alone.

Meryl said, "I'll see to it that you have safe passage to Surmic. No monsters will trouble you—"

"Can't you come? You could help me—"

"No, love. I kept our bargain." She laughed. "I promised to see you wed before I began my adventures, and I've kept my word."

"But that was when you were human." It was hopeless, but I tried anyway. "You're immortal now. Why can't you stay with Rhys and me? You have eternity for adventures."

She shook her head smiling. "Addie, Addie . . . I have work to do. These adventures, they're not play. The fairies need me, and you don't. Not anymore."

She was right. I didn't. I just wanted her.

She put her hands on my shoulders. "But I'll visit often. When you least expect me, I'll be there—and when you most expect me too. Your children will know me well. It's been a long while since a human child has had a fairy godmother, but your children will have me, and your children's children will too. And I'll be with you when there's trouble. Visible or invisible, I'll be with you—and Drualt will as well. One or two merry spirits will always be standing by."

I had to make the best of it. "You'll tell me of your adventures?"

She nodded. "And I'll know about yours. As you conquer the monsters, I'll cheer and exult over every victory." She laughed. "Dru and I will have a fine time watching you."

The spray from the falls behind her caught the sunlight and surrounded her with a glittering halo. She looked magical and human and healthy and glad. I swallowed my tears. If our parting was bittersweet, at least there was enough sweet to comfort me.

We both opened our arms at the same moment. We hugged long and hard. I had the sense to break the embrace first. I patted her cheek one last time and turned away.

I didn't look back. I took Rhys's hand and faced ahead. He and I would have our own adventures, and I'd be as brave as I could be. Meryl would visit sometimes and tell me her tales. I'd weave her adventures and mine into tapestries. I'd put both of us in them, back to back, Meryl fighting her monsters and I fighting mine. And perhaps one day someone would make up verses about us, and we'd be together again, the two princesses of Bamarre.

The sisters embraced
And then they parted,
Their faces tear-washed.
But they wept no more,
And smiled instead, laughed
At what would come,
Whatever would come, though
Hoping, hoping, someday
To embrace again.

Now, when specter haunts,
Or dragon flames,
Or ogre attacks,
Or gryphon descends,
Bamarre fights on,
And the timid march
With the strong.
The tailor, the cook,
The farmer, the queen—
From village, from field,
From castle, from wood—
Bamarre, land of heroes,
Fights on.

Step follows step.
Hope follows courage.

Set your face toward danger.
Set your heart on victory—
Victory for Bamarre!

—From the closing of the epic poem
Two Princesses